AF226213

April Blossoms

Annie Seaton

The Enchanted Village 5

This is a work of fiction. Characters, institutions and organisations mentioned in this novel are either the product of the author's imagination or, if real, used fictitiously without any intent to describe actual conduct.

Copyright © Annie Seaton 2026

Published by ASA, Nambucca Heads, N.S.W.

The moral right of the author to be identified as the author of this work has been asserted.

ISBN 9781764495745

Dedication

As always, to Ian.

Also by Annie Seaton

Daughters of the Darling
From Across the Sea
Over the River
By the Billabong
Beneath Still Waters
Under Darling Skies

A Bec Whitfield Mystery
Bowen River
Shadows on the Shore
Storm Season
Dark Waters

The Catherine Snowden Series
The Forest Keeps
The Drowning Hour
The Witching Hour

Enchanted Village Series
A Magic Christmas
January Joy
February Frolics
March Magic
April Blossoms
Mayday Magic
Midsummer Magic
Harvest Magic

The Happy Outback Hotel (2026)
Outback Strangers
Outback Secrets
Outback Dreams
Outback Hearts

Outback Spirit
Outback Promise
Outback Horizon
Outback Silence
Outback Whispers
Outback Flame

Duckinwilla Days
Coming Home
Secrets and Surprises
Wishes and Whispers
Chasing Dreams
New Beginnings
All Together Now

Home to the Outback
Lucy
Angie
Jemima
Isabella

Porter Sisters Series
Kakadu Sunset
Daintree
Diamond Sky
Hidden Valley
Larapinta
Kakadu Dawn

Others
Whitsunday Dawn
Undara
Osprey Reef
East of Alice
One Summer in Tuscany
Four Seasons Short and Sweet

Follow the Sun
Ten Days in Paradise
Deadly Secrets
Adventures in Time
Silver Valley Witch
The Emerald Necklace
A Clever Christmas
Christmas with the Boss
Her Christmas Star
The Emerald Necklace

The Augathella Girls Series
Outback Roads
Outback Sky
Outback Escape
Outback Wind
Outback Dawn
Outback Moonlight
Outback Dust
Outback Hope
Boxed Sets
Augathella Girls 1-4
Augathella Girls 5-8

Augathella Short and Sweet Series
An Augathella Surprise
An Augathella Baby
An Augathella Spring
An Augathella Christmas
An Augathella Wedding
An Augathella Easter
An Augathella Masquerade Ball
Boxed Set
Augathella Short and Sweet 1-3
Augathella Short and Sweet 4-7

Sunshine Coast Series
Waiting for Ana
The Trouble with Jack
Healing His Heart
Sunshine Coast Boxed Set

The Richards Brothers Series
The Trouble with Paradise
Marry in Haste
Outback Sunrise
Richards Brothers Boxed Set

Bondi Beach Love Series
Beach House
Beach Music
Beach Walk
Beach Dreams
The House on the Hill Boxed Set

Second Chance Bay Series
Her Outback Playboy
Her Outback Protector
Her Outback Haven
Her Outback Paradise
The McDougalls of Second Chance Bay Boxed Set

Love Across Time Series
Come Back to Me
Follow Me
Finding Home
The Threads that Bind
Love Across Time 1-4 Boxed Set

Bindarra Creek Series
Worth the Wait
Full Circle

Secrets of River Cottage
A Clever Christmas
A Place to Belong
Hearts in Harmony

Chapter One

The village looked like something from a postcard—honey-stone cottages clustered around a green, an ancient church spire pointing towards a pale April sky, daffodils blooming in cheerful defiance of the lingering cold. It should have been charming.

Olivia Morrison hated it on sight.

She pulled her car to a stop outside what the rental agency had identified as Primrose Cottage and sat with the engine running, gathering herself. Through the windscreen, she could see the cottage waiting—smaller than the others, tucked at the end of a row, with a garden that should have been blooming but looked strangely dormant. Even the daffodils seemed subdued here, their yellow heads drooping.

Perfect. The cottage looked as miserable as

she felt.

The drive from London had taken nearly three hours, which was two hours and forty-five minutes longer than she'd needed to spend second-guessing herself. She'd turned the car around twice on the M40 before deciding she was committed, and spent the remainder of the journey practising what she was going to say to Hugh.

She had quite a lot to say.

Lower Thistlewick. She'd found it on Facebook, of all places. Hugh's Facebook profile, to be precise. His posts over the past year had been increasingly cheerful: photos of Emma smiling, shots of the village green in various seasons, and worst of all, pictures of him with *her*. Joanna Hartwell. Joanna, who apparently painted watercolours, volunteered at the school and wore her hair in a way that looked to her as though she was trying to look younger. Joanna, who appeared in photo after photo with Hugh's hand at the small of her back, with Emma laughing at something she'd said, with all three of them looking for all the world like a family.

A family that had never suffered any loss.

Four years ago, it had been Sarah with Hugh and Emma. And now she was dead. Sarah had been gone four years. They'd only been in the village a short time before Sarah fell ill.

Four years.

She had stared at those photographs until her eyes watered. She'd grouped them by occasions, and they seemed to be endless. Christmas in front of a tree Olivia didn't recognise, Emma in a new Halloween dress she'd probably chosen with Joanna's help, a birthday dinner to which Olivia had not been invited and had not, until she saw the photos three days later, even known was happening.

Hugh had posted it all publicly, as if none of it was shameful. As if none of it would hurt Olivia.

As if four years were long enough.

She cut the engine and sat in the sudden silence. Outside, a robin landed on the garden wall of the cottage across the lane and regarded her with a beady gaze. She returned the look, her gaze as judgmental as the robin's.

She'd arranged the cottage rental through Mrs Willoughby, the owner, via email. One month, she'd requested. Just a month to visit, to check on Emma, to make sure her niece hadn't forgotten her mother entirely. Mrs Willoughby's responses had been warm but oddly cryptic.

Primrose Cottage will be perfect for you. That one she had read twice, uncertain whether it was reassurance or something more.

I do hope you'll find what you're looking

for. That one had made Olivia frown. She knew what she was looking for. She was looking for signs that Hugh was making a terrible mistake. Signs that Emma was confused, that she needed her aunt, that someone ought to be paying attention to what this woman was doing to Sarah's family.

She got out of the car.

The front path was narrow, edged with stone, and the front door was painted a cheerful yellow—or had been once. Now the paint was peeling, revealing grey wood beneath. The brass knocker, shaped like a primrose, was tarnished to the colour of old pennies. Everything about the cottage seemed tired.

The key was where Mrs Willoughby had said it would be, under a terracotta pot by the door. The pot was empty, the soil inside dry and crumbling despite the damp spring air. She retrieved the key and let herself in.

The air inside the cottage was freezing.

Not just cold from being unoccupied—not the stale chill of a room that needed airing. This was a biting cold, the kind that came up from the ground and settled in your bones. She stood in the hallway for a moment, surprised that even inside she could see her breath misting in the air.

She dropped her overnight bag and went immediately to the thermostat. The heating should have been running for hours. But when she pressed the buttons, nothing happened. The display didn't change. The radiators, when she touched them, were stone cold.

'Brilliant,' she said to the empty hallway. 'Just absolutely bloody brilliant.'

She explored quickly, trying to ignore how her freezing fingers were already going numb. The sitting room—small, crowded with mismatched furniture—held a fireplace with an iron grate that looked as though it hadn't seen a fire in a very long time. Olivia touched the mantelpiece, and her fingertip came away dusty, though the rest of the room seemed clean enough. The kitchen was old-fashioned, with an Aga that radiated a faint warmth. She sighed; at least one room had a bearable temperature. A scrubbed pine table with two chairs sat beneath a window overlooking a back garden that was entirely bare, with not a tree or a flower to be seen. It was not the sort of garden you would expect in a village like this, nor in a cottage named for a flower. It must have been a rental for a long time.

She made her way upstairs, rubbing her arms. Two bedrooms and a bathroom filled the top floor. The main bedroom had a large iron-framed bed with a quilt that looked comforting from across the room and proved, when she sat on it, to be as cold as everything else in the cottage. The second bedroom contained a single bed, a small chest of drawers with a window that looked out over the lane, through which she could see the other cottages glowing with warmth and life.

Olivia sighed and went out to unpack the car; one overnight bag and the box she'd put together for Emma with loving care.

The photos of Sarah. Emma's baby book, the one Sarah had filled in with love, every milestone recorded in her looping handwriting. She stood there looking at Emma's early drawings that she had meant to bring here for years. Sarah would have loved to have seen them.

Pushing those thoughts away, she explored the bottom floor of the cottage. Through the kitchen was a conservatory. She stepped into it and stopped.

The space should have been beautiful—all

glass walls and high glass ceiling, built across the back of the cottage, letting in floods of pale April light. It was the kind of conservatory you imagined, filled with tumbling greenery, with jasmine climbing up the framework and pots crowding every surface and the space filled with the smell of earth and greenery.

Her eyes widened. Every plant inside was dead.

Brown and withered, some collapsed entirely from their pots, others still standing but with their leaves papery and crumbling. Whatever had grown here—and it must have been beautiful once, given the number of pots, the careful arrangement of shelves and hooks and hanging baskets—was now dust and dry sticks. She touched a leaf, and it crumbled between her fingers.

The smell was musty and cold, as though the cottage had been empty for a long time.

'What on earth happened here?' she said to the empty room. 'What is wrong with this place?'

She pulled out her phone to call Mrs Willoughby, whose number she had noted in case she couldn't get into the cottage, and checked for a signal. Of course, there was none. She'd need to find a landline or drive back to the main road. Restless and frustrated, she returned to the sitting room and tried to work the fireplace instead. The wood basket was full, properly full, as if someone had stocked it for her arrival. The kindling was dry. She found long matches in a box on the mantelpiece.

The first one sparked, caught…and went out.

She tried again. The same, a brief flare, then nothing, the flame dying as if the cold air itself were snuffing it.

Again. Again. One after another, the

matches sparked and failed. There was no draught, no particular cold in this corner. There was simply no reason for it.

'This is ridiculous.'

The sitting room door, which had been standing open when she came in, swung slowly shut.

She stared at it. Then at the dead fireplace. Then at the thermostat on the wall, still displaying twenty degrees. With a cross grunt, she went in search of warmth.

She found every blanket in the cottage— three in the airing cupboard, the quilt from the main bedroom, a heavy throw from the sofa— and made herself a bed on the sitting room sofa. She pulled the blankets over her head and tried not to think about how dark it was getting outside, or how isolated this felt, or how she hadn't told anyone where she was going because she'd known they would have tried to talk her out of it.

* * *

Olivia woke to a knock at the door; she must have dozed off despite the cold. The light had changed completely—evening now, the sitting room was filled with deep blue shadow, the village outside bright with cottage lights. She extricated herself from the blanket nest and opened the door to find an elderly woman standing on the path with a covered basket.

White hair swept into a soft bun, eyes a warm grey-green that missed very little, Mrs Willoughby studied her with a quiet, knowing look. 'Hello, Lily.

'Mrs Willoughby?' she said. 'And it's Olivia Morrison, not Lily.'

A pause, then a small, almost amused smile. 'Of course. Olivia.' She tilted her head slightly. 'But to your family… you're Lily. Aren't you?'

Olivia's gaze slipped past her, fixing on

nothing. No one had called her that in years, not since Sarah. It had been Sarah first—small, determined, her tongue stumbling over Olivia until Lily had settled and stayed. Then Hugh. Emma. The name carried forward, softened by use, by love.

Something tightened low in her chest, sudden and sharp. Not quite grief, not quite anger—something more instinctive, a recoil she couldn't smooth away. 'Yes, they do.'

Mrs Willoughby's voice cut gently back in. 'Well then, Lily, if I may… I thought you might need some supper. Travelling days can be exhausting, and I suspected the heating might be giving you trouble.'

'The heating isn't working. And none of the matches will catch. And every plant in the conservatory is dead.' Lily heard the whiny tone in her voice and tried to soften it. 'I was going to ring you, but I couldn't get a signal.'

'No, the signal does struggle in this corner of the village. May I come in?' Mrs Willoughby gestured, and Lily stepped aside.

She set the basket on the kitchen table—Lily could smell soup, something herby and rich, and bread, and something sweet that might be apple cake—and then she turned to survey Lily.

'You're here about Hugh and Emma,' Mrs Willoughby said.

Not a question.

'I'm here to visit my niece. And to check that she's being properly looked after.'

'And you disapprove of Joanna Hartwell.'

Lily's jaw tightened. 'I don't know Joanna Hartwell. I've seen her in photographs. I think that four years is rather soon to be moving on from losing your wife. I think that behaving as though everything is perfectly cheerful, posting photographs on Facebook, introducing new women into your daughter's life—I think that's not enough time. *That's* what I think.'

Mrs Willoughby tilted her head. 'What makes you think Hugh has forgotten Sarah?'

'He's seeing someone new. Emma is calling her by her first name and is clearly attached to her. They look like a family.'

'And that bothers you?'

'Of course it bothers me. Sarah was my sister.' The words came out harder than Lily intended. She forced her voice to soften again. 'My sister was my best friend. We talked every day. I watched her get the diagnosis and go through the treatment, and I watched her die, and now four years later, her husband is posting holiday photographs with another woman, and her daughter is smiling in them, and yes. It bothers me. Of course it should.'

Mrs Willoughby said nothing for a moment. She was looking at Lily steadily, but her expression held neither judgment nor sympathy.

'And so, you've come to do what, exactly?' she asked. 'To make Hugh feel guilty for healing? To use Emma's love for her mother as a reason to disapprove of Joanna? To insert yourself into their lives and remind them that there's another way things could have been?'

The words were quiet, but they landed hard. Lily opened her mouth to object and found, to her own irritation, that she couldn't quite manage it.

'I've come to make sure Emma is all right,' she said finally.

'I'm sure you believe that.' Mrs Willoughby moved to examine the thermostat, pressing the same buttons Lily had tried hours ago. Nothing happened. She pressed them again, unconcerned. 'I should warn you about Primrose Cottage. It's particular about its guests. Rather particular, in fact.'

'What does that mean?'

'It means the cottage responds to the state of your heart as much as to the state of the central heating.' Mrs Willoughby said this in the same tone she might use to say the bin goes out on Tuesdays. 'All the cottages in Lower Thistlewick have their own quirks. Personalities, one could even say. They help the people who stay in them, but only when those people are willing to be helped. If you arrive carrying anger and bitterness and the intention to cause harm, you'll find the cottage rather less cooperative than it might otherwise be.'

'You're trying to tell me this cottage is cold because it doesn't like me.' The woman was crazy.

'I'm saying the cottage doesn't like why you're here. The anger you're carrying. The story you've told yourself about Hugh and Joanna and what their happiness means.' Mrs

Willoughby moved to the conservatory door and looked through the glass at the dead plants within. 'The conservatory reflects the state of things. When a guest arrives with an open heart, it blooms. When they arrive as you have—' She left the sentence unfinished.

'That's completely mad,' Lily said. It was better than saying 'you're completely mad'.

'Probably.' Mrs Willoughby turned back to her. 'Nevertheless, here you are. Cold and alone in an uncooperative cottage because you've come with the intention of disrupting people who have worked very hard to rebuild their lives.' She paused. 'I knew Sarah too, you know. And I can tell you with complete certainty that she would be horrified by what you're planning.'

That hit differently. Lily felt it land in her chest like something physical.

'You don't know what I'm planning.'

'Don't I?' Mrs Willoughby's voice remained gentle. 'You're planning to make Hugh feel guilty for finding love again. You're planning to remind Emma of her grief in ways that will make her feel disloyal for having accepted Joanna. You're planning to use your position as Sarah's sister as a kind of moral authority—to decide what's respectful and what isn't, what's appropriate timing and what isn't. And underneath all of that—' She paused again, and now there was definite compassion in her voice. 'Underneath all of that, you're punishing yourself. For not being there when Sarah needed you. And punishing Hugh for managing to heal when you haven't been able to.'

Lily's mouth hung open; she couldn't speak from the tightness in her throat.

'I'll leave you to settle in,' Mrs Willoughby said, picking up her empty basket. 'The soup is good, it'll warm you. There's bread and cake in the basket as well. And I'd suggest you think carefully, not tonight, perhaps, but soon, about why you're really here. The cottage will keep teaching you until you learn the lesson. It's rather persistent.' She paused at the door. 'Come to Rose Cottage if you need anything. Three doors down. Red door. You can't miss it.'

The door closed behind her.

Lily stood alone in the kitchen and listened to the silence of the cottage pressing in around her. She could almost hear it chastising her. That old woman had planted crazy thoughts in her head, too.

* * *

She ate the soup standing at the Aga, not bothering with a bowl, spooning it directly from the saucepan because the kitchen was the only room with any warmth and she needed both hands on something hot. The soup was exceptional—thick and full of vegetables.

She thought about Mrs Willoughby's words while she ate. The strange things she'd said; how she'd been critical of Lily. How dare she?

What did she know?

You're punishing yourself.

Am I? She'd examined her reasons for making this trip so many times that she no longer trusted her own judgement. She'd convinced herself it was about Emma. About holding Sarah's memory.

I have a right to be here.

As Sarah's sister, she needed to be sure that the people Sarah had loved were holding her in their hearts and memories.

But Hugh's words were echoing too, from the phone conversation last year when she'd called to question whether it was appropriate to be posting photographs with Joanna quite so publicly.

You weren't here,   Lily. During those eighteen months, you weren't here. He'd been controlled about it, not shouting, but controlled in a way that was worse than shouting. *I held it together. For Emma, for Sarah. I made sure we kept living. And now that I've found something to live for again, you want to take that away because the timeline doesn't suit you.*

She'd hung up. She'd told herself he was being unfair.

She hadn't been able to make herself ring back.

The truth, which she'd buried under four years of righteous anger, was simpler and uglier. During those eighteen months of Sarah's illness, Lily had visited perhaps a dozen times. A long weekend here, a couple of days there. She'd sent meals through delivery services. She'd called several times a week. But she hadn't moved back to help. It would have been easy to take extended leave from the marketing firm where she'd finally achieved a senior partnership. But she hadn't been there for the daily reality of it—the chemotherapy appointments, the nights when the pain was bad, the mornings when Sarah couldn't manage the stairs, the school pickups and homework and the business of keeping Emma's life as normal as possible while everything around it was collapsing.

She'd told herself Hugh was managing and that she'd have been in the way. She believed Emma needed stability, not an aunt who cried every time she saw Sarah growing thinner.

But the real reason had been simpler and uglier still. She'd been afraid. Afraid of watching her sister die. Of being there for it, close up, without the safe distance of a motorway between them. She'd visited enough to convince herself she was doing enough, but not enough to actually have to face it.

And then Sarah had died, and Lily hadn't been there. Not at the end. She'd been in London, at work, because Sarah had seemed stable and the prognosis had given them another few months, and the partnership presentation was that week, and she'd thought—

I thought there was more time.

There hadn't been more time. There was never more time. Sarah had died on a Tuesday afternoon in October, with Hugh holding her hand and Emma at school, and by the time Lily had driven down, Sarah was already gone.

She set the saucepan down. Pressed both hands flat against the Aga's warm surface and let herself feel the heat.

She hadn't been there. She'd abandoned her sister during those eighteen months, and she hadn't been there at the end, and four years later, she still couldn't sleep through a night without dreaming about it. Lily still couldn't look at a phone without thinking she should ring Sarah, and still couldn't pass a florist without thinking Sarah would love those colours.

And four years later, she still hadn't found a way to make peace with any of it.

And Hugh, apparently, had. Hugh had found Joanna, and Emma was happy, and the village was beautiful, and their lives were continuing in ways disrespectful to her beautiful sister.

Lily finished the bread, started on the apple cake, and tried not to hate herself too much for her thoughts.

* * *

She went to bed when it became clear the heating wasn't going to cooperate tonight. She piled every blanket in the cottage onto the bed—the quilt, the sofa throw, both blankets from the airing cupboard, her own coat across the foot for extra weight—and changed into the thermal pyjamas she'd had the foresight to bring.

Sleep was slow to come, which gave her too much time for memories. She lay in the dark and found herself back in the hospital, to last year's visit when Sarah had been having what turned out to be her final round of treatment. She'd been thinner than Lily had expected. The camera had lied; it was possible to look well in a photograph and actually be very ill. Lily had walked into the ward, seen her sister and had had to hold herself very still and not react.

They'd talked for three hours. Old stories, mostly. Childhood summers. Their parents. The fun they'd had growing up together. The time Sarah had taken a dare and climbed onto the school roof, and had to be talked down by the caretaker. About the time Lily had permed Sarah's hair; it had been an abysmal failure.

Sarah had laughed every time she looked in the mirror. She'd retaliated and dyed Lily's hair; Lily had come out of that looking like a tortoiseshell cat. They'd talked about Emma, about how funny she was, about how Hugh was managing. They hadn't talked about the prognosis. They hadn't talked about what was ahead.

Sarah had held Lily's hand. 'I know it's hard for you to be here. I know you can't always get away. That's all right, Lily. I know you love me. That's enough.'

She'd meant it kindly. But Lily had heard it then, as she heard it now, as an accusation she deserved.

She must have fallen asleep eventually, because she woke to the unmistakable sound of the bedroom door closing.

Lily sat up and looked at her phone; it was three a.m. The room was pitch dark; she could see nothing. There were no streetlights in the small village. But she knew the door had closed; she'd heard the latch clicking.

She shivered as her bare feet touched the cold floor and hurried across to the door, turning the knob.

Locked.

She tried again, rattling it, putting her shoulder to it. The door didn't move. It wasn't stiff, and it wasn't swollen with damp. It was simply, firmly, locked, with her on the inside and the key on the small hook by the door where she'd hung it before bed. She'd left the door open, foolishly hoping that the warmth from the kitchen might rise to the top floor.

She reached for the key. It wasn't there.

'What the hell,' Lily said to the darkness. 'What in the actual—'

Outside, the village was entirely silent. Even the wind had dropped.

Lily stood in her thermal pyjamas in a locked bedroom in a freezing cottage in a village she didn't know, and she thought about Mrs Willoughby's voice saying the cottage will keep teaching you until you learn the lesson, and she thought about Hugh's voice saying you weren't there, and she thought about Sarah's hand in hers in that hospital room.

I know it's hard for you. That's all right. I know you love me.

She went back to bed. She pulled the blankets over her head. And in the deepest part of the night, in a cottage that had locked her inside her own room and stripped the heating away and left her cold and alone in the dark, Lily Morrison finally started to cry.

Not the controlled crying she'd allowed herself over the past four years, the brief and private grief managed in her own flat with the curtains closed. But the ugly, heaving kind. The kind that came from somewhere deep.

She cried until she was empty. And then, hollowed out and exhausted, she slept.

When she woke in the morning, grey light was coming through the curtains and the bedroom door stood wide open, as if it had never been shut.

Chapter Two

Lily woke to pale sunlight streaming through the bedroom window and the door standing wide open.

She lay still for a moment, staring at the door. Properly open, swung back against the wall; she must have been dreaming. Her neck ached, and her face felt tight after her serious crying jag. She sat up slowly, climbed out of bed and closed the door. She tried the door handle from both sides. It turned without resistance. She checked the hook where she'd hung the key. The key was there.

'Right,' she said to the door. 'I'm going to forget that happened.'

The bathroom taps barely trickled, as she managed a brisk wash in cold water, changed into clothes she'd brought for exactly this purpose—a good wool dress, tights, her proper shoes rather than the boots she'd worn yesterday—and examined herself in the bathroom mirror. She looked exactly as she felt—red-eyed, pale, and washed out.

She had her mother's cheekbones and her father's stubborn jaw and Sarah's eyes. That last had always been a peculiarity—they'd come from no known relation, that particular shade of pale blue that photographs never quite captured. On Sarah they'd looked soft. On Lily they looked watchful.

I know you love me, Sarah said in her memory, from that hospital room. *That's enough*.

'Not today,' Lily told her reflection. 'Today I'm going to church.'

* * *

Easter Sunday in Lower Thistlewick had clearly been an eventful day. As Lily walked the lane to the village green, she encountered the evidence from last weekend—windows still strung with yellow ribbon, front gates wrapped in greenery, daffodil arrangements in pots on porches. Someone had installed a trail of painted wooden eggs along the wall on the way to the churchyard.

The April morning was bright and cold, with early spring brightness but none of the warmth. The sunshine was brilliant, but the air still held a chill. Lily kept her coat buttoned to the collar and her scarf wound twice around and walked briskly, telling herself she was cold, and she was *not* anxious.

She was here to check on Emma. She didn't want a confrontation. She would attend the morning service, see that Emma appeared well and *genuinely* happy—not just Facebook-photograph happy—and make her presence known calmly and with love. As the aunt, who had every right to be part of Emma's life.

She told herself this all the way to the church and tried to believe it.

The church sat at the corner of the green where the lane curved, its Norman tower weathered silver-grey, the stones of the churchyard worn smooth and mossy. The lychgate was wreathed in ivy with new spring leaves coming through. Lilies stood in pots on either side of the church door, white and stark in the cold air.

People were gathering outside, chatting together. Families in their best clothes, grandparents being guided carefully over the uneven path, children chatting happily. The noise was pleasant, the Sunday morning sounds that Lily had grown up with and had not revisited as an adult.

She scanned the crowd, and her heartbeat quickened. There they were, and Emma was laughing.

A happy, full-throated laugh—just like Sarah's—her head thrown back, laughing at something a woman beside her had just said. Joanna Hartwell, recognisable from Hugh's photographs but different in person—warmer-looking, less composed than in the images, her dark blonde hair escaping from the hair clip.

Beside them, Hugh.

Lily hadn't seen Hugh in person for two years. He looked different. Better, she was forced to admit—less hollowed out than during the illness and the years immediately following. He'd always been a slight man, fine-boned, and Sarah had always teased him about his hair. His hair was longer now, curling a little at the collar, and he had colour in his face.

He looked like a man who had come out the other side of losing his wife. Emma's mother. Lily's sister.

The ever-present anger surged in Lily's

chest, and underneath it, surprising her, something else. Something that felt strangely like relief. Hugh was all right. Whatever she'd feared in her worst moments—Hugh somehow falling apart without her knowing, Emma struggling in ways the photographs didn't show—that wasn't this. This was a man who was all right.

Which should have been comforting.

But it wasn't. Not yet. Her thoughts churned in confusion.

Without conscious intent, her steps led her towards them.

Emma saw her first, and the laughter died. Her niece's face went through a sequence of expressions: surprise, recognition, something guarded that stayed. 'Aunt Lily?' she said quietly.

Her voice was different. Older. Of course it was. Emma had been eight when Sarah died, ten when Lily had last visited properly. She was twelve now, with Sarah's dark hair plaited over one shoulder and Sarah's eyes in a face that was quickly maturing. Emma was tall for her age. She was wearing a blue spring coat with a small bunch of primroses pinned to the lapel.

'Aunt Lily,' Emma said again, steadier now.

Hugh turned. Surprise crossed his face, and then confusion. 'Lily. What are you doing here?'

'I'm staying at Primrose Cottage. For a month.' Lily kept her voice pleasant, aware of the attention they were drawing. A village church service was an audience whether you wanted one or not. 'I thought it was time to visit. To see how Emma is getting on. To be here for a little while, properly, rather than just phone calls.'

'Emma's doing very well,' Hugh said.

'She's doing brilliantly. She was the star of the Easter play last week.'

'I can see she is doing well. It's a shame I didn't know about the play. I would have come a week earlier.' Lily's gaze moved to Joanna. Then to Joanna's hand, which was very close to but not touching Emma's shoulder—near enough to offer support if needed.

Joanna stepped forward. She extended her hand, her expression open. 'I'm Joanna Hartwell. I'm so glad to meet you properly—Hugh's spoken about you, and about Sarah. Your sister sounds like she was a wonderful person.'

Lily looked at the hand. The moment stretched. Joanna's hand didn't move.

Lily said, without taking the offered hand, 'I know who you are.'

The briefest flicker crossed Joanna's face, and she withdrew her hand with quiet dignity.

Hugh's jaw tightened. Emma's eyes went to the ground, and she scuffed her boots.

The church bells began to ring overhead, deep and insistent. People started moving towards the door. Hugh put his hand on Emma's shoulder and said something quietly to Joanna, and the three of them joined the flow.

Lily followed.

* * *

She took a pew near the back, alone. The church was beautiful, but she refused to look around. Late morning sun came through the stained glass and threw coloured light across the old stone floor, red and gold and a bright blue that landed on the back of the pew in front of her. She looked at the floor. She looked at her hands.

Hugh, Joanna, and Emma had settled near the front in the fourth pew from the altar. She could see the back of Emma's head, the dark plait, the primroses she'd pinned to her coat. She could see the angle of Joanna's shoulder, and Hugh's hand at one point resting briefly on Emma's head.

She looked away.

The vicar was young, a woman, wearing jeans under her vestments. She had a natural warmth at the pulpit and spoke about the choices people made every day. About the past and what it meant to let go. And how you had to choose that.

Lily closed her eyes; it wasn't meant for her. It was simply a coincidence; nobody had known she was coming to church today.

How you have to choose? Lily turned the phrase over. She didn't like that at all.

All around her, the congregation listened. She recognised some of them from the village green on her walk over. One caught Lily's eye with a smile that Lily hadn't known how to return. Mrs Willoughby was two rows in front of her, sitting straight.

The hymns were traditional ones Lily half-remembered from school. She didn't sing. She held the hymn book and thought about Sarah, who had sung everything at full volume regardless of whether she knew the words, who had embarrassed Lily at every school concert and every family Christmas and who had found Lily's embarrassment hilarious. If she closed her eyes, she could still hear her laughing, that same laugh of Emma's before.

Come to church with me, Sarah had said one Sunday morning, years before she got sick, when they'd both been in their twenties, and Lily had been firmly in her phase of dismissing organised religion.

You don't have to believe anything. Just come for the experience of it. Come for the flowers and the singing.

Lily had gone, begrudgingly. She'd refused to sing and had afterwards pretended she hadn't found it moving, even though she had.

She hadn't gone back after Sarah died. It had been too hard. Everything had been too hard.

After the service, when the congregation filed out into the watery spring sunshine and the women with the coffee urn set up their table by the lychgate, Lily made her way over to Hugh. Emma had already been claimed by two other children and was moving away quickly towards the sweet shop. Hugh was talking to an older couple, and she waited until they'd moved on.

'We need to talk. Properly.' Her tone was brisk.

' Lily.' He looked tired. 'It's Sunday.'

'I know. I'm not trying to ruin anyone's weekend.' She kept her voice down, aware of the parishioners around them. 'I just want you to understand that I'm not here to cause problems. I'm here because I love Emma. I'm here because I miss Sarah. I'm here because I should have come sooner, and I didn't, and I'm—' She stopped. The word sorry was there, almost there. She couldn't quite say it. 'I'm trying,' she said instead.

Hugh looked at her for a long moment. She'd known him for fifteen years, had watched him fall in love with her sister, marry her and be so thoroughly happy with her that Lily had sometimes felt like a third wheel just being around them. She'd watched him during those eighteen months when Sarah was ill, watched him holding himself together through sheer stubbornness for his daughter's sake. She knew his face and his every expression well.

' Lily,' he said. 'You can't just arrive and expect—'

'I know,' she said. 'I know I can't.'

'We've built something here as we've healed. Emma's happy. She's doing well in school, she has friends, and she has stability now. She has Joanna. And whatever you think about that, it's been good for her. It's been very good for her.' He paused. 'Please don't come in and upset that.'

'I won't.'

'That's easy to say.'

'I know that too.'

He looked at her again and then let out a soft sigh. 'Come to the bookshop tomorrow afternoon. Emma will be there after school. Come and see her properly. Don't ambush us at church.'

'All right.' She hadn't expected the invitation. 'Thank you.'

Hugh looked across the churchyard to where a smiling Joanna was talking to a group of women.

'She's not replacing Sarah, Lily,' Hugh said quietly, not looking at her. 'I want you to know that. Nobody's replacing anyone. Emma knows who her mother was. We talk about her all the time. She's everywhere in our lives, Sarah is. You just don't know that because you haven't been here.'

Hugh walked away before she could answer, but she had heard the anger in his voice.

* * *

Lily walked back to Primrose Cottage alone.

The church bells had stopped. The village was settling into the Sunday-noon quiet that follows morning church.

She let herself into the cottage and, despite the sunshine, found it even colder than when she'd left.

She tried to open the sitting room door. It

was locked.

'Oh, for heaven's sake,' Lily said.

She tried the bedroom door. Locked. The bathroom. Locked. The conservatory door was locked, which was particularly annoying because the conservatory had a bench and at least had the decency of being glassed-in and sunny. It might have been marginally warmer than the hallway.

She was trapped in the hallway of a rented cottage, unable to reach any of the furniture or blankets or, more importantly, the soup she'd been looking forward to from the basket Mrs Willoughby had left.

'Mrs Willoughby said the cottage doesn't care for unkind thoughts,' she announced to the walls. 'And you're right, I had unkind thoughts this morning. I was rude to Joanna. I didn't shake her hand when she offered it, and that was—that was small of me.' All was quiet and still. 'And I upset Emma by turning up unannounced, I could see it, and that wasn't the plan. The plan was to be calm and reasonable, and I wasn't calm and reasonable.' She paused. 'But I also don't think locking me out of my own rooms is the answer.'

Good God, she was talking to walls now.

The hallway had a bare wooden floor, a narrow windowsill, a single coat hook and nothing else whatsoever. Lily sat on the floor with her back against the wall and drew her knees up. Her wool dress was not designed for sitting on the floor, but she had no other option.

She thought about Emma's face when she'd seen her. How quickly her laughter had stopped. That careful, bland expression that a young girl should not have.

She thought about Joanna's hand, extended and withdrawn.

She thought about Hugh's angry voice.

She'd brought Emma's baby book in that box. She'd had this image in her mind. Presenting it, of sitting with Emma and going through it together, looking at Sarah's handwriting, remembering. She'd been so certain it would be what Emma needed, a way of maintaining the connection, of ensuring Sarah wasn't forgotten.

But Emma hadn't looked like she was in any danger of forgetting. She had looked like someone who'd found ways to carry grief that didn't crush her. At twelve years old, she had achieved what Lily at thirty-eight hadn't managed: a way of living alongside loss rather than letting it overwhelm you.

That knowledge sat in Lily's chest like a cold stone.

She'd been so certain that Emma needed

rescuing.

And Emma, clearly, did not.

Who needs rescuing here? said a voice very much like Sarah's, and Lily put her face against her knees and tried to ignore it.

She lost track of time. At some point, she heard a key in the lock, and the front door opened to admit a draught and Mrs Willoughby.

'I see,' the older woman said, observing Lily shivering on the hallway floor.

'I was locked out of every room.'

'Yes. The cottage does that.' She held out her hand and helped Lily up. 'Come along. You're coming to Rose Cottage for supper. And I'm going to tell you some things you need to hear, and I want you to try very hard to listen without arguing, which I suspect will be difficult for you, but I have faith that you can manage it.'

'I'm not normally this difficult,' Lily said.

'I know you're not.' Mrs Willoughby guided her towards the door. 'Come. There's roast chicken. That will help more than you'd think.'

Lily took one last look back at the cottage doors, still locked, still resisting. She had a strange feeling, standing in that cold hallway, that the cottage was not unkind. That it was, in its peculiar way, paying attention.

'Fine,' she said to it. 'But I expect the heating to work when I get back.'

She could have sworn the hallway got half a degree warmer. Or perhaps not. Perhaps it was her who was finally starting to thaw.

Chapter Three

Rose Cottage was three doors down from Primrose Cottage, just as Mrs Willoughby had said in her emails. It had a red door and window boxes that should have been dormant in late March but were somehow blooming with early crocuses in three colours: purple, cream, and yellow. The front path was swept clean. Warm lamplight glowed through the sitting room window.

Mrs Willoughby had her key out before they'd even reached the gate.

'In you come,' she said, opening the door, and the warmth hit Lily like a wave.

She almost wept with relief, but she didn't; she'd spent enough emotional energy for one day, but it was close.

The hallway smelled of roasting chicken and

something floral—not perfume, not air freshener, more like real flowers in bloom. The walls were lined with coats and hats, and one enormous umbrella stand full of walking sticks in various states of age. Photographs crowded every available wall space.

'Shoes off,' Mrs Willoughby said, and Lily obliged. 'Through here.'

The sitting room opened off the left side of the hallway, and if Primrose Cottage was cold and unwelcoming, Rose Cottage was its exact opposite. Two sofas, neither matching, both deeply worn and clearly comfortable, sat adjacent to each other. Books everywhere—not in careful rows but stacked and doubled, with slips of paper marking places and notes tucked between spines and one bookshelf that was just a haphazard pile of reading material. A large fireplace with a real fire burning in it, wood and flames, and the soft creak of burning.

A cat occupied one of the sofas. It was large, orange, and very old, and it regarded Lily without interest.

'That's Edmund,' Mrs Willoughby said. 'He'll warm to you eventually. Sit, sit. I'll fetch tea, and then we'll have dinner.'

Lily sat in the armchair that didn't have Edmund in it and let the warmth seep back into her bones. The fire made small comforting sounds. From the kitchen came the sounds of Mrs Willoughby, competent and unhurried.

The photographs drew her eye. They crowded every surface—framed pictures on the mantelpiece, arranged on the bookshelves, grouped on a small table by the window. She recognised the village in many of them: the green, the church, the bridge over the millstream. Weddings and christenings and harvests and winter markets and summer fêtes, a whole village life across many years.

Hugh and Emma were in several photographs. Hugh outside the bookshop, the Chapter & Verse sign newly painted behind him, grinning. Emma at maybe nine or ten, wearing a beekeeper's veil and looking both scared and happy, a honeycomb frame held at arm's length. There was Hugh and Emma together at what appeared to be a Christmas market, both in scarves, Emma eating something steaming.

She looked for a long time at Emma in these photographs. Emma laughing, Emma concentrating, Emma performing some task with seriousness. She looked well. She looked—

Content.

In the more recent photographs, there was Joanna.

Not many of her, but she was there. Standing with a group of women at an outdoor market, paintings visible on a stand behind her. Sitting next to Emma at a table, both of them looking at something off-camera with the same expression—absorbed, amused. And one, on the mantelpiece, that Lily forced herself to look at properly—Hugh and Joanna and Emma, taken outdoors somewhere, autumn trees behind them. Not posed, not smiling for a camera. Emma was in the middle, leaning slightly against Joanna, the easy acceptance of a child who doesn't think about it. Hugh had his arm around Joanna's shoulders. They were all looking at something to the left of the frame, caught in a moment of shared attention.

A family. Lily looked at the photograph and saw, clearly, that they were a family.

It should have made her angrier. She was surprised to find it made her something else—something that hadn't quite finished forming but felt like the beginning of understanding. A half smile tilted her lips.

'Tea.' Mrs Willoughby set a tray on the table between them—proper bone china, a good pot, milk in a small jug. And sandwiches that Lily hadn't asked for and badly needed: good bread, proper butter, fillings that had been thought about. She ate two before she could stop herself and was reaching for the third when she caught herself and slowed down.

'I'm sorry. How rude of me,' she apologised.

'You were hungry,' Mrs Willoughby observed.

'I didn't have lunch. The cottage had locked me out of the kitchen.'

'Ah. That would do it.'

They sat for a moment in the warmth and the firelight. Lily was still tired, still emotionally exhausted from the morning. But the warmth and the food and the ordinariness of being in a room with another person were making her feel better.

'You saw Sarah in those photographs,' Mrs Willoughby said. Not a question.

'Yes. Emma looks like her. The eyes.'

'She does. She has Sarah's colouring and Hugh's stubbornness.' A smile. 'She's a wonderful young girl. Very funny. Very certain of herself. And a brilliant organiser. You should have seen her last week, organising the Easter egg hunt for the children.'

Lily shook her head. 'She looked wary when she saw me this morning.'

'Yes. She would. From what she'd told me, she's seen you at funerals, brief Christmas visits, and on a video call or two. She knows you're her aunt, she knows you loved her mother, and she knows—children always know—that you disapprove of something here.' Mrs Willoughby sipped her tea. 'Yes, that makes her wary. Because Emma loves her life here. She loves Joanna. And she doesn't want to feel guilty about that.'

'I didn't come here to make her feel guilty.'

'I know. But intentions and reactions aren't always on the same page.' Mrs Willoughby set down her cup. 'Tell me about Sarah. Not about her death—I know about that, we had that conversation, she and I, in this very room. Tell me about her when she was well. When she was herself.'

Lily blinked. No one had asked her that in four years. People had offered condolences, had said kind things about loss and time and healing. Not one person had simply asked her to talk about Sarah as a living person.

'She was,' Lily started, and stopped, and tried again. 'She was ridiculous, actually. She was the funniest person I've ever known in my entire life. She had this ability to find the absurdity in everything—not from a mean-spirited point of view, but she could find the comedy in any situation, and she'd start laughing, and then you couldn't help laughing too.' Lily looked down at her hands, clenched together, and smiled. 'Even if you'd been furious a minute before.' She paused. 'Sarah was also very stubborn. More stubborn than me, which is saying something. If she decided something was true, you could argue until you were blue in the face. She'd nod and look sympathetic and do exactly what she'd decided to do anyway.'

'Hugh would recognise that description.'

'She drove him mad with it. He adored her for it.' Lily looked at the fire. 'She was a primary school teacher. Year Three, mainly. Sarah was an extraordinary teacher. She had this special rapport with children—she could see exactly what each child needed and provide it without making it look like special treatment. Emma got that from her. That instinct for people.'

'What was she afraid of?'

The question caught Lily off guard. 'What?'

'Everyone's afraid of something. What was Sarah afraid of?'

Lily thought. 'She was afraid of being ordinary, I think. Of living her life and not having made a difference. She used to say she didn't need to be famous or important. She just needed to have made things better in her small corner of the world. She thought that was everyone's responsibility—to make things better wherever they found themselves.' She looked at her hands again, flexing her warm fingers. 'She was better at it than most.'

'And what are you afraid of, Lily?'

The room was very warm. Edmund had migrated from the far sofa to the arm of Lily's chair. He purred beside her.

'That's not a fair question,' Lily said.

'No. But it's the right one.'

Lily didn't answer immediately. She scratched behind Edmund's ear and watched the fire as his purring got louder. The clock on the mantelpiece ticked. Outside, the village was quiet.

'I'm afraid that I failed her,' she said at last. 'That I wasn't there for her when she needed me, and that I can't take it back, and that there's nothing I can do now that will make it right. And so, I came here instead to do something, even something wrong, because doing nothing was—' She stopped. 'Because doing nothing for four years has been destroying me, and I had to do something. Even if the direction was wrong.'

Mrs Willoughby said nothing. Just listened.

'Hugh was right this morning. I wasn't

there. I visited, but I wasn't there. I had a life in London that I couldn't seem to put aside, that seemed—I told myself it was important. The job. The career. All of it seemed very important at the time, and now I can't remember why any of it seemed to matter, but I can remember exactly what it felt like to watch Sarah's number ring on my phone, and I'd let it go to voicemail because I was in a meeting. Because I was always in meetings.'

'You were frightened,' Mrs Willoughby said. Not an excuse, just a statement.

'I was a coward.' The word was ugly and accurate and releasing to say out loud. 'I couldn't bear to watch her suffer. I'd go down for a weekend and come back a mess. For days. And I looked for—and found—reasons to go less often. And when she died, I wasn't even there, I was in London, I thought there was—' Her voice steadied itself with difficulty. 'I thought there was more time. And then there wasn't.'

'And you've been angry at Hugh for four years because he healed. Because he found a way forward that you couldn't.'

'Yes.' The admission cost something, the saying of it out loud. 'I told myself I was here for Emma, that I was worried about her, that this was all about protecting Sarah's memory. But mostly I've been furious that he could— that he got to heal and I didn't. That he found Joanna and Emma adjusted, and life went on in ways it apparently isn't allowed to go on, and I'm still stuck in the same place I was in October four years ago.' She looked up. 'And I drove three hours to come and make his life difficult because I couldn't bear that he'd found a way to be happy and I hadn't. What sort of a person am I?'

The fire crackled. Edmund purred louder.

'That's a very honest thing to say,' Mrs Willoughby said.

'I'm tired of not saying honest things. Keeping it inside hasn't worked.'

'No. It generally doesn't.' The older woman refilled her teacup and paused, looking at the photographs on the mantelpiece. One of Hugh and Joanna and Emma with the autumn trees. 'Can I tell you something about Joanna?'

'If you want to.'

'She came to this village the way most people come to this village—needing something she couldn't quite name. She's gentle, and she's gifted, and she's been very careful with her relationship with Emma. She is very aware that Emma had a mother she will always love and that her role is not to replace her. She talks about Sarah. Asks Hugh to tell her stories about Sarah because she wants Emma to see that the women in her life can hold Sarah's memory with respect. She and Emma look at photographs together sometimes. She's asked Emma to teach her Sarah's recipe for lemon drizzle cake because it was Emma's favourite and Sarah used to make it every Sunday.' Mrs Willoughby met Lily's eyes. 'Joanna is not erasing your sister. She's helping a twelve-year-old girl carry her grief. And that's exactly what Sarah wanted.'

Lily's eyes were burning. She looked at the fire until she had control of her tear ducts. 'I can see it,' she said quietly. 'When I look at those photographs of Emma, I can see that she's all right. That she's more than all right. That something has been very carefully tended here.' She paused. 'It makes it harder, in a way. It would be easier for me to change things if something was wrong.'

'Yes,' Mrs Willoughby said. 'It always is. If something were wrong, you'd have a purpose.

You'd have something to fix. As it is, there's nothing to fix here. There's only yourself.'

The words sat there. True and quietly devastating.

'So, what do I do?' Lily asked. 'What do I do with four years of guilt and anger and the fact that I wasn't there and can never be there and can't take it back?'

'You forgive yourself. Eventually, in small pieces, you forgive yourself.' Mrs Willoughby said it simply. 'And in the meantime, you do what you came here to do. Not the thing you told yourself you came for, but the real thing. You become part of Emma's life. You let Hugh be happy without it being an accusation. You let Joanna be kind to you, and you accept that her kindness doesn't cancel Sarah—it's just kindness for its own sake.'

'And the cottage?'

'The cottage will help. When you let it.' Mrs

74

Willoughby stood and moved towards the kitchen. 'Dinner's nearly ready. And afterwards, I want to hear more about Sarah. The funny stories. She sounds like the kind of person who deserves to be talked about properly, not just grieved over.'

Lily sat by the fire for a moment more. Edmund moved from the arm of the chair to her lap. He was very heavy. He was also, she discovered, extremely warm.

'All right,' she told him. And the room. And the cottage three doors down. 'All right.'

* * *

Dinner was roast chicken with all the trimmings—roast potatoes in goose fat, carrots and parsnips, homemade gravy, and a bread sauce that Lily hadn't had since childhood.

They ate at the kitchen table, which was smaller than the dining room table and more cosy, and Mrs Willoughby talked about the village. About Hawthorn Cottage and the couple who'd stayed there in autumn and come out the other side of something complicated into something better. About Violet Cottage and what had happened in the spring. About a "fairy"—just ask Emma about Fern—wedding that was just coming up on May Day. About the village history, which stretched back further than the Norman church suggested.

'The bridge,' Mrs Willoughby said, gesturing in its general direction. 'Every wedding in this village takes place on the bridge. Traditional. Not official—the legal part happens in the church or the registry office. But the ceremony, the vows, are always on the bridge over the millstream. The village considers it properly married when the bridge has witnessed it.'

'That's charming,' Lily said, and meant it without irony, which surprised her.

'Will you still be here on May Day? Fern and Callum are getting married on the bridge.'

'My rental is for the month.'

'Good. Emma's a bridesmaid. She's been planning her dress with Fern for weeks. Forget-me-nots, she tells me, which seems right.' Mrs Willoughby poured more wine—a good Burgundy that had appeared from somewhere. 'There'll be a planning meeting on Wednesday, at Rose Cottage, if you'd like to come. Emma will be there. It might be a gentler way to spend time with her than the church this morning.'

'I managed that very badly.'

'You managed it as someone who is carrying what you're carrying. The question is what happens next.' Mrs Willoughby looked at her steadily. 'You could leave. Go back to London. Decide this was a mistake. Or you could stay and do the harder thing.'

'Stay and actually face it.'

'Stay and let the cottage teach you. Let the village be what it is. Let Emma show you who she is now rather than who you've been missing. And perhaps—' A pause. 'Perhaps tell Hugh the real reason you weren't there during those eighteen months. Not the justifications. The real reason. I think it will help you both.'

'He'd think I was making excuses.'

'He might. Or he might recognise it. Hugh was afraid, too, during that time. He was terrified and exhausted and doing everything alone. He might be more understanding than you expect.'

Lily turned her wine glass slowly between her palms. 'I do owe him an apology.'

'Yes. And Emma. And Joanna, who extended her hand and had it ignored, which is not the kind of thing that people forget even when they forgive.'

'I know.'

'But not tonight. Tonight, eat and rest and let the cottage settle a little. Tomorrow will be time enough.' Mrs Willoughby picked up the apple tart that had appeared on the counter. 'Pudding?'

* * *

Lily walked back to Primrose Cottage when the village had gone properly dark, and the only sound was her own feet on the lane and something—an owl, probably—somewhere in the trees beyond the church. The early spring air was cold and clear, and there were more stars above than she'd ever seen before.

She stood for a moment at the gate before going in. The cottage looked different in the dark—not as old, the honey-stone catching the moonlight, the yellow paint on the door almost cheerful rather than peeling. She could see the silhouette of the conservatory at the back, the glass catching the sky.

She let herself in.

The hallway, when she stepped into it, was—not warm, exactly. But less arctic. The sitting room door opened when she tried it. The bedroom. The bathroom. Even the conservatory, whose plants still stood in their dry and sorry state, but seemed, perhaps, marginally less hopeless than this morning.

Lily stood in the middle of the hallway.

'I'm sorry,' she said to the cottage. To the cold air. To the bare walls and the dead conservatory and the memory of her sister that seemed to live here more vividly than she'd expected. 'I'm angry and frightened, and I've been managing my grief very badly for four years. I wasn't there for Sarah when she needed me, and I can't take that back, and I don't know how to forgive myself, but I understand why that's the work I have to do now. I understand that what I was planning to do here was wrong.'

She paused. 'I'm going to try. I'm going to try to do better. To be the aunt Emma deserves rather than the one I've been. To let Hugh be happy. To understand that Joanna isn't an enemy.' Another pause. 'I'm going to be terrible at it, probably. But I will try.'

The cottage was quiet.

Lily went to the thermostat and pressed the buttons, and heard—faintly, from somewhere behind the walls—the sound of the heating system beginning, with great reluctance, to engage.

She went to bed in a cottage that was still cold but slowly warming, pulled the blankets up to her chin, and thought about what Mrs Willoughby had said about Sarah. That she talked about her with Hugh, that Emma kept photographs, and that the lemon drizzle cake recipe had been used. That Sarah was still present in the life of this house and this village and these people in ways that had nothing to do with guilt and everything to do with love.

She'd been so frightened they'd forgotten.

They hadn't.

Before she slept, Lily got up and went to the box she'd brought and took out the baby book. She sat on the edge of the bed with it in her lap, looking at Sarah's handwriting—the careful entries for the early months, the cheerfully illegible scrawl once Emma had started moving and life had accelerated beyond easy record keeping. First word: *Dada*. Eight months. Very pleased with himself. First steps: disaster. Fell into the bookcase. Very unconcerned. First day of school: I cried. Emma did not.

Lily sat with the book for a long time.

Then she put it back in the box carefully, where Emma could look at it when she was ready, if she wanted to. Not as ammunition. Just as a gift.

She went back to bed. Through the window, the stars were still up there, bright and beautiful. The heating system made a periodic rumbling noise that was somehow reassuring.

In the conservatory, if she'd been looking, a single shoot of something green was pushing its way up through the dry and exhausted soil of a pot that had given up hope several months ago.

But Lily wasn't looking. She was asleep.

And in the morning, she would try.

Chapter Four

Monday morning dawned grey and drizzly—proper April weather. Lily woke to find Primrose Cottage a little less hostile than the day before. The heating was working at approximately half capacity, which meant the house was merely chilly rather than icy. The water ran when she tried the taps, though it was barely lukewarm. The doors opened without resistance.

She took it as encouragement.

After a breakfast of toast made on the Aga—the only cooperative appliance in the house—Lily decided to explore the village properly. If she was going to be here a month, she should at least know where things were. And she needed to think. The cottage was too small for the kind of thinking she had to do, and last night's revelation—that she'd been punishing herself, that she'd been punishing everyone—sat heavy in her chest. She needed air and space to think and settle.

She pulled on her waterproof jacket and headed out into the drizzle.

* * *

Lower Thistlewick was small enough that you could walk the perimeter in twenty minutes. The village green dominated the centre, with its ancient stone cross, and over the millstream was a graceful stone arch bridge. Lily stopped on the bank and looked at it. Old stone, worn smooth where hundreds of hands had rested on the parapet. The millstream below was running clear and quick from recent rain, the sound of it steady and reassuring.

She'd have to cross it, she thought, before she was done here. One way or another.

Cottages clustered around the green like

friends, each with its distinct character but all sharing the honey-stone construction and slate roofs that spoke of centuries of history. Lily walked past Rose Cottage—Mrs Willoughby's, with its red door and blooming window boxes, the crocuses undeterred by the drizzle. Past what a discreet sign identified as Hawthorn Cottage—Joanna's, presumably, and she made herself look at it squarely rather than sideways. It was a handsome cottage with a climbing rose over the door that would be spectacular in summer. A watercolour painting was propped in the front window, presumably put there to dry. Bright blues and greens, the millstream captured with what looked like real skill.

She kept walking.

Past Pippin's Nook, where someone had painted the name on a cheerful sign by the door and left a pair of muddy boots under the porch. The Old Swan pub closed but promising a noon opening. A small shop advertising *Everything You Need* in the way of a village shop that had been providing everything you needed for several generations. A café called The Cosy Cup with steamed windows and the smell of fresh baking drifting out through the door.

And on the far side of the green, bow windows bright in the grey morning was Chapter & Verse.

Hugh's bookshop.

Lily stood across the green and looked at it. She'd been avoiding this side of the green, taking the long way around since yesterday, but she made herself stop now and look properly. The bow windows were perfectly dressed—a hand-painted sign hung above the door. The shop window had a display she was too far away to read, but the arrangement of it suggested care. Time spent. A person who actually loved what they'd created.

She thought about what Hugh had said at the church.

I finally did it after she died. Took me two years to get up the courage. He'd been talking about the bookshop, she knew now. Two years to gather himself up and build something from the rubble. Two years of being alone with a grieving child in the village, running on empty, and he'd somehow managed to build this.

She should go in. Talk to him properly. But she was aware that she'd already used up her store of courageous conversations for the week, and she had an appointment here this afternoon anyway—tea at four, as he'd said yesterday outside the church. Emma after school. One step at a time.

She turned away from the bookshop and headed up the hill that overlooked the village.

* * *

The path beyond the church was muddy

from the overnight rain, winding upward through bare trees and early undergrowth, the kind of English hillside that looked bleak in early April and would be beautiful in May. Lily climbed it, the rain soft on her face, the village falling away below.

From the top, among a stand of pine trees, she could see for miles. The village below, scattered around its green like something from a model—the church tower, the pub sign, the bright red of Mrs Willoughby's door, the millstream catching grey light as it curved under the bridge. Fields spreading out in every direction, the Cotswolds rolling to the horizon in shades of green and brown and the pale gold of old grass not yet renewed by spring.

It was beautiful.

Peaceful.

The kind of place that made you want to live in the moment.

Sarah would have been up here within twenty minutes of arriving, Lily thought. Would have been pointing at things and naming them and finding poetry and laughter even in everything, despite the grey light.

Those last few months of her illness, when she could still talk properly, she'd shown Lily photographs Hugh had sent from the village. They'd been sitting in the hospital day ward while Sarah had a transfusion, and she'd handed Lily her phone.

Look. Look at this view. Emma found this path on her third day here—Hugh said he could hardly get her back down again.

And there had been a photograph of the village from somewhere up high, taken on a clear day, everything glowing golden. Sarah had looked at it the way she looked at things she couldn't have yet.

Promise me you'll visit them, she'd said.

After. Promise me you won't let Hugh and Emma become strangers. Promise me you'll be there for them.

And Lily had promised. She'd held Sarah's hand and promised and she had meant it at the time.

I didn't keep my promise.

She sat on a fallen log among the pines and let herself face it fully, without the anger of loss that had been cushioning her denial for four years. She'd meant to keep it. Her intent had been real.

But the first year she'd been drowning in her own grief and the grief had made her avoid Emma and Hugh, and the second year the avoidance had turned into distance, and by the third year she'd told herself she was giving them space, and now it was four years and she'd spent those four years protecting herself from her own failure by being angry at Hugh for not needing her.

Sarah had known. That was what Hugh had said last night at Mrs Willoughby's dinner: *She told me to tell you that she understood why you couldn't be there. That she never blamed you.*

Lily put her face in her hands and wept. Not the ugly heaving crying of the night before— that had been from somewhere too deep and too long dammed up for that again. This was quieter.

She cried until the rain got heavier, and it would be difficult to walk down the hill. Wiping her face with her sleeve, she looked out at the view Sarah had loved from a photograph and said quietly, 'I'm sorry. I'm going to try to make it right. I know I can't undo it. But I'm going to try.'

The pines creaked gently in the wet wind. Below, Lower Thistlewick went about its Monday business.

* * *

Lily walked back to the village around noon, red-eyed and still damp despite the waterproof, and headed for The Cosy Cup with a sudden need for something hot. She pushed the door open.

The café was small and warm and smelled of coffee and something baking that involved cinnamon. A woman behind the counter looked up.

'You must be Lily. Primrose Cottage?' She had a round, kind face and flour on her apron. 'I'm Margaret. Sit anywhere—I'll bring you something warm.'

Lily sat at a window table and watched the rain streaking the cobblestones outside, and tried to decide how she felt about being in a village where everybody already knew who she was.

Actually, she didn't mind it. She'd been

anonymous in London for fifteen years, and it wasn't as appealing as it sounded.

Margaret brought tea and a wedge of cake that smelled delicious. 'Lemon drizzle. My Monday bake. I'll warn you, it's addictive.'

Lily bit into it and nodded. It was excellent—sharp, sweet and slightly sticky.

'Emma's favourite,' Margaret added, refilling a sugar bowl at the next table. 'Sarah's recipe, originally. Hugh gave it to me the first year they were here. He said Emma needed to be able to eat it and have her mum's kitchen feel close.'

Lily set down her fork. 'He gave you Sarah's recipe.'

'Yes, he said it was the kind of recipe that should be shared. That it'd been made with love and ought to keep being made.' Margaret settled against the counter. 'He's a good man, Hugh. He built himself back up through sheer stubbornness and love for that sweet child. Joanna's been good for him. Good for Emma too.'

'I'm beginning to see that,' Lily said. 'I wasn't ready to before.'

'You're ready now. That's what matters.' Margaret nodded towards the window, where the rain was easing. 'He's in the bookshop all day if you want to see him this afternoon. Mondays, he's usually restocking.'

Lily looked at the bookshop across the green. The bow windows. The hand-painted sign. The shop her sister had dreamed about and her sister's husband had built in her memory.

'Maybe I will,' she said.

* * *

The door of Chapter & Verse opened with a tinkle of the bell, and Hugh looked up from behind a stack of boxes with surprise that quickly changed to wariness before taking on a blandness that was out of character for the kind Hugh who had loved her sister.

' Lily.'

'I'm not here to argue,' Lily said immediately. 'I'm here because this is a beautiful shop and I wanted to say that. And because I wanted to apologise for yesterday. The church. Not taking Joanna's hand. I was very rude, and I'm sorry.'

Hugh set down the book he'd been holding. 'You didn't have to come here for that.'

'I did, though. It was unkind. She offered her hand, and I didn't take it, and that was small of me.' The bookshop was warm and smelled of old paper, and Lily let herself look around properly—the shelves running from floor to ceiling, the arrangement of sections, the little handwritten recommendation cards tucked beneath various spines. 'Did you write all these?'

'Emma helps. She's decided she has very strong opinions about crime fiction.' The bland expression was easing, replaced by something more like the man she'd known fifteen years ago. 'She reviews thrillers for the shop newsletter. Very seriously. I have to remind her the audience is mostly retired villagers, not the Booker Prize committee.'

Lily smiled, the first genuine smile she'd managed in two days. 'That sounds exactly right. Just like Sarah had strong opinions about everything.'

'Emma is exactly like her mother in that respect.' Hugh moved a box off the nearest chair. 'Sit, if you want. I'll put the kettle on.'

She sat. He disappeared to the back room and soon returned with two mugs of tea and a plate of biscuits.

They sat among the books with their tea, and

the rain ran down the windowpanes.

'I was supposed to come for tea this afternoon,' Lily said. 'And see Emma after school.'

'You can still come. Though Emma might find it less alarming if it's not a surprise visit.' Hugh wrapped both hands around his mug. 'She's cautious. Been cautious since you turned up at church. But she's also twelve, and forgiving is easier at twelve than it is for adults. If you come this afternoon and you're—you, rather than the version of yourself you were on Easter Sunday—she'll come round.'

'The version that ignored Joanna's handshake and implied she was a bad influence.'

'That one, yes.' His tone was even. 'Joanna was fine, by the way. She's had worse. She understands grief makes people snap better than most.'

'She was much kinder than I deserved.' Lily turned her mug between her palms. 'I owe her an apology too.'

'In time. Don't try to fix everything in one day.' Hugh looked at her steadily. 'We've all got time. We're not going anywhere. Come for supper tonight.'

* * *

Lily returned at five. The flat above the bookshop was reached by a staircase at the back, narrow and steep, and the door at the top had a note taped to it in uneven handwriting: *Knock first. The cat bites.*

She knocked.

Emma opened the door. She was in her school uniform still, blazer discarded, holding a biscuit and looking at Lily carefully. 'Hi.'

'Hi.' Lily held up the paper bag. 'I brought madeleines. JK from the sweet shop said they help everything. I've been testing the theory.'

Emma considered this. 'Does it work?'

'I think so. Jury's still out.' Lily held the bag towards her. Emma took it, examined it, and stepped back to let Lily in.

The flat was small and full of warmth—bookshelves everywhere, Emma's drawings on the refrigerator, and a cat asleep on the sofa. The kitchen smelled of the pasta sauce Hugh was making, and Joanna was sitting at the table with a sketchbook and the whole place had the comfortable disorder of a happy home.

Joanna looked up and met Lily's eyes.

'I want to apologise, Joanna,' Lily said, before she lost her nerve. 'For yesterday at the church. I was rude and unkind.'

Joanna set down her pencil. 'Thank you. I appreciate that. Apology accepted.' She smiled gently. 'Would you like to sit?'

Lily sat. Emma arranged herself cross-legged on the sofa next to the cat, opened the madeleine bag, and ate one with a glance at Hugh.

'Only one before supper,' he said.

The 'Yes, Dad,' came with an eye roll and a sweet smile at Lily. Lily's heart thawed a little more.

The pasta was ready twenty minutes later, and they ate at the kitchen table, which was a tight squeeze for four people. Emma talked about school—a project about local history, a friend's birthday, the drama of a sports match that had apparently been decided under controversial circumstances. Hugh listened and asked questions, and topped up Emma's water glass without being asked, and Lily noticed how uncomplicated their relationship was. She blinked away a tear.

Emma looked directly at Lily. 'Did you know Mum used to make pasta like this?'

'I didn't know. She never cooked pasta

when we were growing up.'

'She learned after she and Dad got together. She said she made it wrong for years before she got it right. She showed me how once, but I kept forgetting to salt the water.' Emma twirled pasta around her fork with great concentration. 'Joanna showed me again last year. I'm better at it now.'

Joanna and Hugh both looked at Lily carefully, checking how she'd take this.

Lily tried to respond better than her reaction yesterday. 'Sarah was a terrible cook when we were young,' she said. 'She once made scrambled eggs that I'm fairly certain qualified as a biohazard.'

Emma giggled. Hugh laughed, a genuine, deep laugh. 'She never told me about the eggs.'

'She made me swear never to mention it.' Lily looked at Emma. 'Your mum was many, many wonderful things, but a natural cook was not one of them. She worked very hard to become a good one.'

'She was brilliant at it by the time she was sick,' Emma said seriously. 'She made the best roast dinners. Dad still tries to make them like hers, and they're never quite the same.'

'Mine aren't that bad,' Hugh offered, without much conviction.

'They're good,' Emma said, kindly. 'Just different.'

Lily walked home in the dark with rain just starting again and felt, for the first time in four years, that she had done something right.

* * *

The sweet shop was still open when she passed, light spilling warmly across the wet lane, and Lily pushed the door open and went inside.

JK looked up from behind the counter.

'Hello, again. You look better than this morning. Something has shifted, yes?'

'Several things,' Lily admitted. 'I had dinner with Hugh, Emma and Joanna. We had some good conversations.'

What was it about this village that everyone cared about you?'

JK came around the counter. 'Sit. One last madeleine. Before I close up.'

They sat at the small table by the window, and the rain came on properly outside, and JK told Lily about her husband, Jacques—about his loss, but about the sort of man he was. How he'd laughed. How he'd been terrible at directions and refused to admit it.

'Do you miss him still?' Lily asked.

'Every day. But differently now. Like a—a warmth rather than a wound.' JK turned her madeleine between her fingers. 'In the beginning, missing him was sharp. Like glass.

Now it is more like sunlight through water. Still there, always there, but soft. And I am glad for the years, rather than only angry for the loss.'

Lily walked back to Primrose Cottage with the madeleines and a head full of thoughts. The cottage greeted her with less hostility than it had in days—the door opened easily, the sitting room was *almost* warm, and when she went to the conservatory, she found that one plant—just one—was no longer quite dead. A single green shoot pushing up through brown earth, defiant and hopeful.

She touched it gently. 'You're as stubborn as I am.'

That evening, she sat in the conservatory with a cup of tea and tried to imagine what Sarah would say if she could see her now. Not the Lily she'd been on Sunday, hard and cold and looking for evidence of betrayal, but Lily as she was now: soft and tentative, trying to understand.

Sarah had known. That was what Hugh had said: *She understands. She'll come round eventually. Be patient with her.*

'I'm working on it,' Lily told the cottage. The green shoot. The ghost of her sister seemed very present in this silence. 'I don't know how to let go, not completely. But I'm starting to understand that holding on hasn't been working. And that you—' she looked at the shoot, pale and stubborn in its pot of exhausted earth '—you're managing to grow despite everything. So perhaps I can too.'

The cottage was quiet. But the single green shoot stretched a little taller, reaching towards the light.

Lily watched it for a long time and felt something inside her shift. The first tiny crack in the wall she'd built around her grief.

The beginning of letting light in.

Chapter Five

Wednesday arrived wet and cold—typical early April weather. Lily woke to rain drumming on the cottage roof and the sound of wind rattling the windows. Primrose Cottage, whilst still not exactly welcoming, had at least stopped working against her. The heating worked well enough to keep the chill at bay. The taps ran properly. And in the conservatory, three more plants had begun showing signs of life—tiny green shoots pushing through dead earth, stubborn little miracles that she'd taken to greeting each morning the way she might greet a friend.

She spent the morning working on her laptop—emails from her London clients that she'd been ignoring, bills that needed paying, the routine of life that couldn't be avoided just because she was having some kind of crisis in the Cotswolds. Her inbox was a cheerful reminder that the world outside Lower Thistlewick continued as normal. A brief note from her colleague asking when she'd be back.

We've had three new enquiries. The Henderson account wants a meeting.

Lily stared at the Henderson account for a while and thought about the fact that she'd spent fifteen years building a career that she didn't care about one bit.

She filed the emails and closed the laptop.

Around noon, the rain eased enough for her to walk to the village shop for provisions. The woman behind the counter was one of the Pemberton sisters—'Edith Pemberton, how do you do'—who had apparently been running the shop with her sister since 1994 and who told Lily about the village's thirty-seven permanent residents, two seasonal residents, and 'a steady flow of people the cottages bring in, who come needing something and leave having found it, though sometimes it can take a while.'

'The cottages bring people in?' Lily said, transferring a tin of tomatoes and a wedge of cheese into her basket.

'Always have. Ask Mrs Willoughby, she'll tell you the history. Goes back centuries, apparently—people finding their way to Lower Thistlewick in times of difficulty.' Edith Pemberton selected a loaf. 'Take this one. The sourdough's better than the white this week— the baker's been experimenting.' She handed it over. 'You're at Primrose Cottage?'

'I am.'

'Ah. It was quiet for a while before you arrived. The cottages do that sometimes—go quiet between the people who need them.' Edith Pemberton said this as if it were the most ordinary thing in the world. 'It'll be glad you're there. Even if it hasn't shown you yet.'

'It's warming up,' Lily said. 'Gradually.'

'That's usually how it goes.'

* * *

She ventured out again at two o'clock, in her waterproof, to walk the short distance to Rose Cottage.

The planning meeting.

She'd promised JK she'd come, and promised herself she'd try, even when part of her still wanted to retreat into Primrose Cottage's slightly warmer sitting room and pretend none of this was happening. But she'd had tea with Emma on Monday. She'd spent two genuine hours in Hugh's company and not once tried to make him feel guilty. She was slowly making good on the version of herself she'd promised the cottage she'd be.

She knocked on Rose Cottage's red door.

Mrs Willoughby answered. 'Wonderful.

You came.' She drew Lily in out of the rain. 'Everyone's just settling. Let me take your coat.'

The sitting room was packed.

JK was seated in the armchair nearest the fireplace with a plate of madeleines on her lap. Lily recognised Dimity March and her partner, Vivian, from Mrs Willoughby's description, a tall man with kind eyes. An older woman with Edith Pemberton, introducing herself as Francis, was the sister Lily hadn't yet met.

She didn't recognise the young woman in jeans and a soft jumper until she spoke. It was the vicar. 'We need a contingency plan,' she said to Mrs Willoughby. 'If it rains at noon on May Day, the bridge becomes difficult. The stone gets slippery. We should have the covered option ready.'

'The green has the pergola,' Mrs Willoughby said. 'We could rig a canvas if needed. But I think it will be fine. The village tends to produce reasonable weather for important occasions.' She said this as if it were a given.

In the corner, with a plate of biscuits, was Emma, who looked up with a serious expression as Lily crossed the room.

'Hi, Aunt Lily.'

'Hi, Emma.' Lily forced herself to seem relaxed. She sat in the chair on the other side of the room rather than the one nearest Emma, giving her space, not wanting to push the issue. 'How was school?'

'Fine. We're doing a local history project. I'm writing about the bridge.' Emma's manner was still careful. 'Did you know it's been in the same place since the thirteenth century? The current stones are newer, but it's been a bridge for eight hundred years.'

'I didn't know that. That's remarkable.'

'The millstream changes, but the bridge stays,' Emma said. 'Mrs Willoughby says that's what the village is like. Things change, but the important parts stay.'

Before Lily could answer, the door opened. The couple who arrived were clearly the guests of honour—they walked in confidently with huge smiles.

'Sorry, sorry!' The woman—Fern, the bride, Lily gathered—shook rain from her coat. 'We stopped to help Alf move a barrel, and it took longer than expected. He has very strong opinions about where to put the barrels.'

'He really does,' said the man beside her—Callum, tall and easy-going. He had bright eyes and was holding Fern's hand.

'Fern! Callum!' Emma threw herself at Fern, bursting with excitement.

Fern caught her and hugged her back. Lily ignored the small shaft of jealousy that tried to surface.

'My bridesmaid! How's the slow-walking practice going? Mrs Willoughby's been timing you, I hear.'

'I'm very dignified now. I've been practising with a book on my head.'

'Excellent. We need at least twenty seconds of dignity. After that, you can be your usual whirlwind self again, sweet Emma.' Fern looked around the room and grinned. 'Hello, everyone. It's so good to be back! Thank you for giving up a wet Wednesday. Callum and I are overwhelmed by how many are happy to help.'

'It's what our village does,' Mrs Willoughby said, settling the room. 'Now. We have a great deal to cover. Vicar Sarah, do you want to start with the ceremony planning?'

* * *

The planning discussion that followed was a

lively kind of planning Lily had never experienced before.

Vicar Sarah had detailed notes and her strong views about the timing of the bridge ceremony versus the weather risks. Margaret had the wedding cake organised. JK was doing wedding favours—'Madeleines in small bags tied with white ribbon, it is perfectly French and therefore perfect.'.

Dimity had apparently volunteered to write the village newsletter coverage of the wedding.

'You do realise we're guests,' Vivian said. 'A notebook might be pushing it.'

'I'm not going to write in a notebook at the ceremony,' Dimity said. 'I'll be discreet.'

Vivian raised an eyebrow. 'Says the author who always has a notebook.' His grin was wide. 'Would I be telling tales out of school if I mentioned the one you dropped in the bath the other night?'

Dimity grinned and pulled a notebook from her bag, and tapped him with it. 'You would!'

Lily smiled at the easy rapport between them. Then there was a lovely moment when she caught Emma watching her, and her niece smiled back at her.

Fern was describing the flowers she wanted. 'Wild spring flowers, nothing formal. Primroses, if possible, and forget-me-nots, and I want it simple.' Her voice was firm; she knew exactly what she wanted. 'I don't want fuss. I want to stand on the bridge with my man and choose him. That's all.'

'Well said,' Mrs Willoughby said.

Joanna came in from the bookshop, coat damp; she'd been at the bookshop with Hugh. She slid into the seat beside Emma, shedding her wet coat, and immediately Emma leaned in and whispered something in her ear. Joanna listened, glanced at Lily, and smiled.

Lily looked away. Then back again. The room was quiet around them. The village had gathered around two people's happiness with complete sincerity, offering what they had without being asked, and she thought about what it would be like to be part of something like this. To belong to a place that cared.

She'd been alone in London for four years, managing her grief in her careful single flat, going to work and going home and being perfectly fine from a distance. She hadn't known she was lonely until she saw what the opposite looked like.

' Lily?' Mrs Willoughby's voice pulled her back. 'Would you like to help with the decorations? Margaret could use an extra pair of hands. Friday afternoon, if you're free.'

Emma was watching her.

'I'd like that,' Lily said. 'Very much. Thank you.'

 ***

After the meeting, when people were pulling coats on and collecting umbrellas, Hugh arrived to walk Joanna and Emma home. He caught Lily's eye and nodded to the kitchen, a question in his eyes. Joanna stood with Emma as they said goodbye to Fern and Callum, who were going straight home.

'I'll miss them.' Emma's voice followed them as Lily and Hugh headed for the kitchen.

'I would like to say something,' Hugh began.

'I would prefer to begin.' Lily looked at him squarely, this man who had been her sister's husband and her own sometime-friend and the person she'd been blaming for four years because blaming him was easier than looking at her behaviour. 'I was wrong,' Lily said. 'I told myself I was protecting Sarah, but I wasn't. I just didn't know how to forgive

118

myself for not being there.'

Hugh said nothing. He listened.

'I left you both when it mattered. I know that.' She held his gaze. 'I'm so very sorry.'

Hugh was quiet for a long moment. He looked down at the kitchen floor. Then up at the window, where rain was still running in rivulets down the glass. 'Sarah said something to me once,' he said. 'Near the end. "When I'm gone, be patient with Lily. She'll carry this wrong. She won't know how to put it down".' He looked at Lily. 'She knew you. She knew exactly how you'd handle it.'

Lily let out a breath. 'She always knew me better than I knew myself.'

'She never blamed you.' He paused. 'I was angry after church on Sunday.'

'You were right.'

'Still unkind.' A beat. 'We need to make our peace. For Emma.'

Lily nodded. 'We do.'

'I can't promise to be perfect.'

'No.' A small smile. 'But I can be stubborn.'

Hugh smiled back. 'Emma actually suggested she'd take you on a tour of the village on Saturday. Would you like that?'

'Oh, yes!'

***

Lily walked back to Primrose Cottage in the late evening, the rain finally eased, the village quiet and dark except for the occasional lit window. The cottage door opened easily when she arrived. Inside, it was warm. Not just working-heating warm but genuinely warm, the Aga was going properly, the sitting room fire apparently having taken it upon itself to light while she was out.

In the conservatory, six plants were now showing green, and the primroses were producing buds.

'Thank you,' Lily told the cottage. 'I'm trying. I really am.'

The warmth pulsed in response.

She sat in the conservatory for a while in the warm darkness, looked at the shoots and thought about holding something small and homemade in her hands. About a life that was hers rather than a life that had been designed for her.

It was the first time she'd thought about her future without it feeling like a threat.

Chapter Six

On Friday, Lily went to Margaret's café. The Cosy Cup was everything a village café should be—mismatched chairs at mismatched tables, walls covered in local art with small handwritten price cards, the hiss of an excellent coffee machine, and the general atmosphere of a room that has been providing warmth and good baking for long enough that the warmth has permeated the walls.

'Five minutes,' Margaret said. 'Dimity's already started.' She pushed open the heavy door at the back of the café. They entered a large, light-filled space with workbenches down both sides, materials arranged along both walls.

Lily looked around, wide-eyed. You would never guess this was behind the café. The studio was a converted barn. Light. Workbenches. Greenery laid out.

Dimity looked up from a length of ivy laid out on a long bench. 'Reinforcements! Thank God. My wreaths look like something a badger built. I'm a wordsmith, not a florist.'

'You've done well,' Margaret said and then showed them how to weave, not twist. Turn the frame. Keep it even.

Lily's hands quickly found the rhythm, and she smiled as she worked. Their mother had done something similar. Not wreaths exactly, but the same instinct—the instinct for arrangement, for balance, and for creating. She'd forgotten she'd inherited it. Sarah had laughed, saying it was the only way that Lily had taken after their mother.

'You're good, Lily,' Dimity said.

Lily glanced up. 'I can thank my mother for those skills.'

Dimity added a sprig of early primrose to her own wreath, which was improving. 'My mother is hopeless at anything practical. Vivian can fix anything. Thank goodness, because our cottage needs a lot of TLC.'

'You're improving, Dimity,' Margaret said.

'So,' Dimity said eventually, 'how are you finding the cottage?'

'Warmer than it was. Less hostile.' Lily wove a stem of ivy through a gap. 'It was very hostile when I arrived.'

'Pippin's Nook was hostile with me too. Kept making things cold, or lights would flicker. Drove me absolutely mad until I realised it was trying to tell me something.' Dimity secured her ivy with a twist of wire. 'That I was lying to myself. Pretending I was fine when I wasn't. Trying to be the person I'd been before my accident, rather than accepting that the person I was had changed.'

'Your sight?'

Dimity looked at her steadily. 'Hugh told you?'

'Mrs Willoughby, actually. In passing.'

'It's not a secret. I had a traumatic brain injury. Woke up completely blind. Spent weeks convinced everything was over—my career, my independence, everything. Then I came here to hide from all of it.' She looked around the studio with the fond affection of someone in a place they chose and are glad they chose. 'The cottage wouldn't let me keep hiding. Kept making things difficult, uncomfortable, impossible to ignore, until I finally stopped fighting and admitted I was broken and needed help. And then it started helping rather than obstructing.'

'What did helping look like?'

'Warmth. Little things—a book falling open to the right page, plants blooming at unexpected moments. The feeling of being supported rather than alone.' Dimity turned her wreath, examining it. 'The cottages don't fix you. They create the conditions. You do the actual work. But having that space, that feeling of being somewhere that actively wants you to heal—it makes a difference.'

'I've felt it,' Lily said. 'This week. The cottage is getting warmer as I—as things shift.'

They worked on, finishing late afternoon with a dozen wreaths and twenty feet of garland. Lily looked at what they'd made with something she hadn't felt about work in a very long time: satisfaction. Margaret stepped back. 'Fern will love these.'

'She will,' Dimity said. 'Now, Lily, please come to us for supper. Vivian's cooking.'

***

Pippin's Nook was exactly the kind of cottage Lily had imagined when she'd been

126

planning this trip in London and trying to imagine what a village in the Cotswolds actually looked like. Stone walls, low ceilings, the kind of inglenook fireplace you saw in period dramas and assumed no longer existed in actual homes. A sitting room crammed with books and framed artwork, and a kitchen that smelled of roasting vegetables and garlic.

They ate dinner at a table in the sitting room, rain still running down the window, firelight flickering on the walls.

'What do you do?' Vivian asked Lily. 'In London?'

'Marketing. Mostly corporate. Events, launches, brand work.' Lily turned her wine glass. 'It pays well.'

'But?' Dimity said.

'Was there a but?' Lily looked at her.

'Would you do it, if it wasn't for the pay?'

Lily turned her glass. 'I used to think about

something a change,' Lily said slowly. 'Something I created made rather than managed. A shop, maybe. Plants or handmade things.' She paused. 'Sarah always said I'd be bored by it. That I needed the buzz of London.'

'Did you agree with her?' Vivian asked.

'I thought I did.' Lily looked at the fire. No one spoke. She looked at the fire. 'Now I'm not sure. Maybe she was wrong.'

Chapter Seven

Saturday morning, Emma arrived at Primrose Cottage at nine, in jeans and a sensible coat, her expression full of anticipation. 'Ready for the village tour, Aunt Lily?'

'Absolutely.' Lily grabbed her coat. Jeans, jumper, boots—she'd thought about what to wear more than she wanted to admit.

'Where are we going first?'

'The bookshop. Dad's doing inventory today, but he said I could show you around properly. And then the bridge.' Emma set off down the lane without waiting. 'And then the hill, if you want. I go up there most mornings.'

'I've been up the hill,' Lily said, falling into step beside her.

Emma glanced sideways. 'When?'

'Monday. I walked up through the pines.'

'That's not all the way up. The best bit is another ten minutes past the pines. There's a view from there that Mum would have liked.' Emma said it lightly. 'I found it by myself. Dad doesn't know about it. He's afraid of heights.'

'Your dad is not afraid of heights,' Lily said, surprised.

'He says he isn't. But he goes very pale on the hill and pretends to be interested in the flowers.' Emma kept her face straight. 'I decided that was probably a fear of heights and didn't tell him about the second view. I was being kind.'

Lily laughed. Properly. 'That was extremely kind.'

* * *

Chapter & Verse in the morning was different from the last time she'd called in. Lily stopped in the doorway and simply took it in.

Grey light through the bow windows caught

the spines—blues and greens, worn reds and golds. Books that had been handled, passed on, talked about. The smell of them—constantly read.

It was the sort of bookshop Sarah would have stood in the doorway and said something like "Oh, this is perfect, this is exactly it," and been right.

'Dad!' Emma called into the depths. 'We're here. I'm starting at the children's section.'

'Right-o.' Hugh's voice came from somewhere behind a shelf. 'I'm doing crime. Don't reorganise anything.'

'I'm not going to reorganise anything,' Emma said to Lily, in a tone that suggested reorganisation had previously been an issue between them. She hid a smile. Sarah would have been proud of Emma's confidence.

She led Lily towards the back of the shop. 'This way.'

The children's section occupied the rear left corner, and Lily understood within three steps that it had been made with love. Not just stocked well—though it was stocked well, a carefully curated collection that mixed classics and new releases and things you wouldn't find in the larger chains. The section had been made beautiful. A window seat with cushions. A low rug. A reading lamp positioned at the right height for a child sitting on the floor. Shelves at a child's height.

'Mum's section,' Emma said. She touched a spine, and her fingers rested there for a moment. 'All her favourite children's books. The ones she used to read to me. Dad set it up after we moved here, so I'd always have a place to come and remember.'

Lily looked at the shelves. She recognised some of the titles—books she'd given Emma as gifts over the years, books she'd known Sarah loved, books that had been part of their own childhood and that Sarah had kept and passed on.

'She kept her old ones,' Lily said as she spotted Sarah's childhood copy of *A Little Princess*, the pages yellowed, the spine lovingly repaired with tape at some point. She'd have known that copy anywhere.

'She kept everything. All the ones that mattered.' Emma ran her fingers along the spines slowly. 'Mum used to say that a book someone has loved is different from a book that hasn't been loved yet. That you could feel it in the paper.'

'I think she was right. These ones feel different from the new copies.' Lily rested her hand on the shelf. The softened paper. The give of the spines that had been opened and closed many times, the warmth of a book that has lived in a house and been a part of it.

Sarah was here. In these books. In Emma—her hands, her voice.

Not in this room—she'd never seen this bookshop—but she was in these books. In the girl standing beside Lily, who had her eyes and her hands and her way of speaking about things she loved.

'I come here when I miss her,' Emma said, without drama. 'Sit in the reading corner and read the ones she loved. Sometimes I can almost hear her voice reading them. The way Mum did the different voices—she was terrible at the voices, actually, but she always did them anyway.'

'She did them for me too, when we were children,' Lily said. 'The villain always sounded the same regardless of the book or character.' Emma snorted with laughter.

'Yes! That's exactly it! She gave the stepmother in Cinderella the same voice as the

White Witch. I thought they were the same person for years.'

Lily reached for *A Little Princess*. 'May I?'

Emma nodded.

Lily drew the book from the shelf and opened it. Inside the front cover, in handwriting she would have recognised anywhere, a child's inscription: *This book belongs to Sarah Jane Morrison, aged 8. **PRIVATE. DO NOT READ UNLESS ASKED.***

Beneath it, in adult handwriting, Sarah's: *For Emma. Every girl should know Sara Crewe. Love, Mum.*

Lily's throat closed. She stood there with the book open in her hands, and found she couldn't speak, and didn't try to. Emma was quiet beside her.

'She wrote in all of them,' Emma said. 'Little notes at the front. Different things for different books. Some of them are just—just things she wanted me to know.' She paused. 'When I miss her badly, I read the notes. It's like she knew she was leaving messages for me.'

'She did know,' Lily said. Her voice came out steadier than she'd expected. 'She knew. She knew you'd need them.' She put the book back on the shelf carefully.

'I should have come sooner,' she said. 'I wasn't the aunt you needed. I'm sorry. Truly sorry, Emma.'

Emma looked at her steadily. Whatever she saw in Lily's face seemed to satisfy her.

'Mum said you'd come round eventually,' she said. 'She told Dad you'd find your way here when you were ready. She said to be patient.'

Lily let out a breath. 'That sounds like her.'

'Yeah.' Emma's mouth curved. 'A very

annoying quality in a parent.'

* * *

Hugh was in the crime section, counting stock from a clipboard. They spent half an hour in the shop—Emma showed Lily her recommendation cards, and Hugh pressed books on her with quiet enthusiasm. Lily bought three. It felt right. She had time to read. And the cottage needed the company.

At half past ten, Emma took charge again.

The bridge was their second stop.

It was better in person than Lily's glimpse of it on her morning walk. The parapet was worn smooth where hands had rested. Below, the millstream ran clear and quick, reflecting the grey sky, and the sound of it, steady and unhurried.

'This is where Fern and Callum are getting married,' Emma said, leaning on the parapet. 'Right here, in the middle. Vicar Sarah stands at one end, the bride and groom in the middle, and everyone crowds in on both banks. Mrs Willoughby says you can fit the whole village on the banks if needed. Thirty-seven people isn't that many.'

'What's the tradition? Mrs Willoughby mentioned something about the bridge and weddings.'

'The village considers you properly married when the bridge has witnessed it. It's always been that way. The magic of the village is strongest at the bridge, apparently. Weddings and important things.' She leaned further over the parapet and looked at the water. 'When Mum died, I came and stood here for a long time. I don't know why. It just seemed like the right place.'

'Did it help?'

'A bit. The water keeps going. I liked that it didn't stop.' Emma straightened up. 'Come on.

The hill next.'

* * *

Emma's "the rest of the hill" turned out to be higher. The path climbed past the pines, then higher. Heather, scrub, a second ridge.

The view opened. It was different from the pine grove—wider, taking in not just the village but a long valley to the west, and another hillside opposite.

Emma sat on a flat stone at the top. Lily joined her, breath still catching.

'I come up for sunrise,' Emma said. 'Started after Mum died. Dad was asleep and I couldn't sleep, and I came out really early and walked up here, and it was just—' She gestured at the view. 'Just this. And it kept going. The sun kept coming up. And I thought—Mum would have liked this. And somehow that made it better. Not good, but better.'

Lily followed her gaze and thought about

139

Sarah. Of everything she would have loved and never seen.

For four years, she'd held that gap open, as if closing it meant losing her. Standing here, she saw something else. Emma, living alongside it.

'She would have loved it,' Lily said. 'All of it. And you most of all.'

Emma looked at the valley and was quiet for a long moment. 'Do you think Mum can see it? From somewhere?'

Lily considered giving a careful answer. The one that didn't make promises she couldn't keep.

'Yes,' she said instead. 'I think so. I don't know how or where, but I think people we love don't entirely leave us. I think Sarah is absolutely watching every sunrise with you, even if you can't see her doing it.'

Emma was quiet for a moment. 'I think so too. I didn't want to say it in case it sounded silly.'

'It doesn't sound silly.'

'Joanna says love doesn't disappear. It just changes shape.'

Lily smiled faintly. 'That sounds right.'

Emma turned a dry stem in her fingers. 'She's been careful about Mum. She asks Dad for stories all the time. She learned Mum's lemon drizzle recipe from me and made it last week, and it tasted right. Not exactly the same, but right.'

Lily nodded.

'Emma,' she said. 'Are you really okay?'

Emma thought about it.

'Some days aren't good,' she said. 'Some days I can't breathe properly.' She looked up. 'But most days are. And I've got people. And the hill. And the books. And Mum's notes.' A pause. 'And you. If this is the real you. The one Mum loved.'

'It is me,' Lily said. 'The angry version's gone.'

Emma's mouth curved. 'Good.'

'She frightened me too, to be honest.'

Emma almost laughed. Not quite—a smile that was considering it. 'Okay. Come on. Next stop. JK opens at half ten on Saturdays, and there will be fresh madeleines.'

* * *

JK pressed madeleines into both their hands at the door.

'Ah! You are friends now, yes? This is good. Your mother would be very pleased, Emma.'

'I think so,' Emma said, already eating.

'Sit,' JK instructed. 'I will bring more. You have earned them. Walking the hill on a cold morning earns at least three madeleines each.'

They sat at the small table by the window and ate madeleines and watched the village go about its Saturday, and JK talked about the wedding preparations.

'Alf says the reception should have dancing immediately. I say dancing should come after the food, because dancing immediately on an empty stomach is a recipe for disaster. We have agreed to disagree.'

'Alf's right about dancing,' Emma said. 'You should always dance when you get the chance.'

'This is the wisdom of youth,' JK said. 'I will reconsider.'

By lunchtime, Lily felt lighter than she had in four years.

* * *

They ended up at The Old Swan for lunch, where Alf the publican greeted Emma like a favourite granddaughter and subjected Lily to a series of jokes she could tell had been prepared with her as audience.

'What did the flower say to the bumblebee?' he asked.

'I couldn't possibly imagine,' Lily said.

'Don't be such a buzz-kill!' Alf slapped the counter. Emma groaned. 'Ah, she hates them. That's how I know my riddles are working.'

'That's genuinely terrible,' Emma said, from behind her hands.

'All my best jokes are terrible. Settling in?' Alf asked Lily, pouring drinks.

'Better,' Lily said. 'Once I stopped fighting it.'

'That's the trick.' Alf leaned on the bar. 'My Dorothy always said Lower Thistlewick has a way of finding people when they need finding. And the cottages have a way of making things impossible until you admit what you actually need.' He looked at Lily steadily. 'Lost her six years ago. Took me a long time to stop being angry at everything.'

'What changed?'

'Mrs Willoughby sat me down one afternoon and told me, "Alfred, your wife loved you for thirty years, and she would be absolutely furious at what you're doing with the time she'd have given anything to have." And I thought about that for a week, and then I knew she was right. Dorothy would be absolutely furious.' He pulled himself a half pint. 'She'd want me to run a good pub and tell terrible jokes and look after the village and be glad for the years we had. So, I started doing that. Grief doesn't go. But you learn how to carry it.'

'How long did it take?' Lily asked.

Alf thought about this honestly. 'Three years, maybe. Still have bad days.' He shrugged. 'But I'm glad now, when I think of her.' He disappeared to the kitchen for their food, and Emma looked at Lily across the table.

'He's right, you know,' she said. She lined up the salt and pepper. 'I used to think being happy meant I didn't miss Mum. It doesn't.'

Lily nodded.

Alf brought their meals out. They ate, and talked about the wedding, and about Emma's school project, and about whether it was possible to make it rain on May Day by the whole village worrying about it.

When they left, Lily stood looking down the lane for a moment in the cold April air—at the green and the bridge and the cottages and the church and, at the end of the lane, Primrose Cottage with its yellow door and the garden that was now getting some colour.

'Thank you,' she said to Emma. 'For today. For the tour and the bookshop and the hill and all of it. I've really enjoyed spending time with you.'

Emma considered. 'You can come to the

sunrise view again if you want. Not every morning. But sometimes.'

'I'd like that,' Lily said.

It was, she thought, walking back to the cottage in the late afternoon, a small thing, but the most generous invitation she'd been given in years.

Chapter Eight

The second week settled into an easy rhythm Lily hadn't expected. She woke each morning and went to the conservatory first, before tea, before anything. It had become a kind of habit—checking on the shoots, counting what had progressed overnight. Seven plants were now showing green. Then eight. The primroses in the large pot by the south-facing glass had produced their first flowers, pale yellow and perfect, nodding at her with the certainty of something that had always planned to bloom and was simply now getting around to it.

The cottage was warm. Properly warm. It had the warmth of a house that was being lived in rather than merely occupied.

She was working, too—freelance emails answered, a proposal drafted for a London client she was considering dropping, and having increasingly honest conversations with herself about whether the career she'd built was the career she wanted to continue. She sat at the kitchen table in the mornings with her laptop and the Aga behind her and the soothing sound of the village coming awake outside, and was repeatedly distracted by the view from the window, taking her attention from the document she was supposed to be editing. This would have alarmed her two weeks ago. Now it didn't matter. Now it made her happy.

Emma came on Tuesday after school, and they walked up to the pine grove again, not all the way to the second view, but far enough to sit among the pines and talk. Emma was working on her history project. She asked Lily questions about what Lower Thistlewick might have looked like three hundred years ago, and Lily found herself drawn into the research, the way she used to get drawn into things when she was young and hadn't let go of her natural curiosity.

On Wednesday, she helped in the bookshop for three hours when Hugh had an appointment and wouldn't leave Emma alone in the store. Lily had expected it to be difficult, but it wasn't. She helped a retired professor find a first edition of something obscure, recommending titles she knew and a few she didn't.

When Hugh returned, he looked surprised to find her deep in conversation with two customers about the merits of various walking guides to the Cotswolds.

'You're good at that,' he said, when they'd gone.

'I used to love books. Before I decided to do things that paid better.' Lily ran her hand along a shelf. 'I'd forgotten how much.'

Hugh looked at the shelf and then at her and didn't say whatever he was thinking, which Lily appreciated.

On Thursday, she finally sorted the box she'd brought with Sarah's things. Not the way she'd first imagined—photos set out like proof of something lost.

She sat cross-legged on the sitting room floor and went through it slowly. Emma's baby book, set aside for later. A photograph of her and Sarah as teenagers, terrible haircuts, squinting into the August sun. A letter Sarah had written the Christmas before she got sick—ordinary, full of plans.

She read the letter.

Then she put the photograph of her with Sarah on the mantelpiece, where it belonged.

Not to make a point. Just to have her there.

The hooks on the wall, which had refused to hold anything in those first days, held the frame without slipping.

* * *

Sophie and Daniel arrived on Friday evening.

Lily had heard them mentioned—the couple from Violet Cottage who'd left last month, who'd come broken and gone home healed, and were returning for the wedding. She'd expected them to be people from London who came out for the weekend and stayed city through and through. Two weeks ago, that had been her.

She was wrong.

They arrived in a car that was packed almost to the roof—bags, a potted plant in the back seat that Daniel carried out with more care than he gave to the larger bags, two bottles of wine, and a box that turned out to contain a handmade quilt that Sophie had made for Fern and Callum.

Lily smiled as she listened to their laughter floating into the conservatory from outside

152

Violet Cottage.

Mrs Willoughby had organised a welcome dinner at Rose Cottage. Lily walked down in the early evening to find the sitting room already full—Sophie and Daniel, Dimity and Vivian, Hugh and Joanna, Emma, Margaret and JK. The happy chatter filled the room as everyone talked over each other.

'You must be Lily,' Sophie said immediately, coming across the room. 'Mrs Willoughby mentioned you'd been having an adventure with Primrose Cottage.'

'That's one word for it,' Lily said.

'How is it now? We drove past—it looked beautiful. All the primroses in the garden.'

'It's much better. It was very unhappy with me when I arrived.' Lily glanced at the window. 'I was very unhappy with myself, which the cottage apparently takes personally.'

Sophie laughed, and her laughter held some

surprise. 'Yes. Violet Cottage took everything I was feeling personally. It was relentless about it.' She glanced at Daniel, who was chatting to Hugh. 'We nearly didn't make it. The cottage wasn't the problem—it was us. But it gave us somewhere safe to fall apart, and then somehow the falling apart meant we could start putting ourselves back together.'

'That's what it's been like,' Lily said. 'Though I've been doing more of the falling apart than the putting together, until this week.'

'That sounds about right. March was a falling apart month for us. April was reconstruction.' Sophie looked at her. 'You're here for Hugh and Emma?'

'I came for the wrong reasons. I'm staying for the right ones.'

Sophie nodded as if this made complete sense. 'Good. I can see Emma's been different this week—lighter. That's you being here, I think.'

* * *

Dinner fell into that easy rhythm—conversations blending, stories picked up and passed on.

Dimity and Vivian compared notes with Sophie and Daniel about the village in March and now. Emma insisted on demonstrating her wedding walk, slower than before, chin lifted, hands folded just so. She made it halfway across the room before dissolving into laughter, taking the rest of them with her.

'Dignified,' Hugh said.

'Extremely,' Lily agreed.

JK offered to demonstrate a correct Madeleine-eating technique she claimed was the correct approach. 'You eat from the narrow end. Always. There is no other way.'

Lily noticed Hugh's eye roll, and she and Joanna shared a smile.

Alf arrived with more wine and told four jokes. One of them worked. He looked faintly disappointed. 'I'll have to retire that one,' he said. 'It's lost its appeal now you've laughed.'

Somewhere in the middle of it, Daniel said to Lily, 'What did you do before all this?'

'Marketing. Corporate.' She turned her glass. 'You?'

'Architecture. Still am, just… smaller now.' He glanced at Sophie. 'The cottage had opinions.'

'What did it do?'

'Refused to let me work. Everything crashed. Every time.' He shrugged. 'I took the hint.'

'Primrose Cottage locked me out on my first day there,' Lily said.

Sophie smiled. 'Ours put lavender in bloom in March. And kept making us end up in the same place at the same time.' She looked at

Daniel. 'Very persistent.'

'They like people to pay attention,' Daniel said.

'And then you have to do the work,' Daniel said. 'The cottage can't do it for you. But having somewhere that believes you can heal, that is actively cheering for you—' He paused. 'It matters. It changes how possible the thing feels.'

Lily nodded. She'd begun to understand that.

Later, she carried plates through to the kitchen with Mrs Willoughby. The sound of laughter followed them from the sitting room.

Sophie came in behind her.

'Can I say something?' she said.

Lily smiled. 'Go on.'

'I nearly left Daniel in March. I thought we were done.' She rested her hands on the edge of the bench. 'What stopped me was remembering all the times we'd chosen each other. Not the losses. The choosing.'

Lily was quiet.

'I think grief's like that,' Sophie said. 'You don't stop loving someone. You just decide what to do with it.'

'What do you do with it?'

'You give it somewhere it belongs. Sarah loved Hugh and Emma. You still love her.' Sophie met her eyes. 'So, give it there.'

Lily looked at the plate she was holding, then set it down.

'That's the most useful advice anyone has given me since I arrived,' she said.

From the other room, Emma's laughter rose again—bright, unguarded.

'It makes total sense,' Lily said.

Sophie smiled. 'It did to me too.'

Chapter Nine

Saturday brought an unexpected test.

Lily arrived at the bookshop mid-morning, intending to help Hugh with a delivery. He was there with Joanna and Emma, and the easy domesticity of them together—Hugh making tea, Joanna unpacking boxes, Emma reading in Sarah's corner with her feet up and her shoes off—hit her in a way she thought she'd let go of.

Not anger.

Missing Sarah.

Not the tight, guilty grief she'd been carrying.

Just the *missing*.

Sarah should have been here. Behind the counter. Calling out to Hugh from somewhere between the shelves. Laughing at something that had set off her unique sense of humour. Pressing a book into Emma's hands and saying, "You have to read this one."

Sarah should have seen the bookshop. The life Emma had made inside it. In the village. Her circle of friends and the love they gave her.

Lily stood there with it—how easily Sarah would have fitted here, how completely she would have belonged—and the heart-wrenching reality that she never would.

She didn't move from the doorway.

Her hand rested against the frame; fingers curled into the worn wood. For a moment, she forgot to breathe. The room blurred, just slightly, as everything in it—Emma's voice, the shelves, the light—pressed too close.

Not anger. Not guilt.

Just the loss.

It rose clean and sharp, and she let it fill her.

Her other hand came up, briefly, to her mouth. She closed her eyes, steadied herself, then opened them again. Stayed.

'You all right?' Hugh was watching her from behind the counter, Joanna standing beside him.

'I'll go and make a cup of tea,' Joanna said quietly before she went to the small kitchen.

'I miss her.' Lily's voice shook. 'That's all. Just miss her.'

Hugh was quiet for a moment. 'Me too. Always. Every minute of every day.'

Emma looked up from her book. She'd heard them. She climbed off the window seat and came to Lily and put her arms around her. Hugh's hands went to Emma's shoulders. The three of them stood there for a moment—husband, daughter, and sister—with the loss held between them.

'Mum would have been here every day,'

Emma said finally. 'Reorganising the shelves. Laughing all the time at the way Dad arranged things.'

'She'd have reorganised them continuously,' Hugh said. 'And because I know that, it makes me think, and I've learned to do it well.'

'She'd have been right,' Lily said.

'Infuriatingly so,' Hugh agreed.

Emma let go of Lily and went back to her book. Joanna came through from the back with a tray of tea, setting it down between them. She poured without fuss, then, as she passed Lily a cup, gave her hand a brief, quiet squeeze.

'It's good to have you here,' she said.

Lily nodded, unable to say much more.

Hugh took his tea. Emma turned a page. The shop settled again.

Lily picked up the box of deliveries and began to unpack it, the small, ordinary chore steadying her.

The morning passed quickly.

That evening, Primrose Cottage did something it had never done before.

Lily came home to find the conservatory door propped open—she'd left it closed—and the smell of the primroses drifting through into the kitchen, warm and sweet and unlike anything she'd known a room to smell of in April. She stood in the kitchen doorway and looked into the conservatory, at the thick clusters of yellow flowers in every pot, at the green abundance of a space that a fortnight ago had been dead in every corner.

She'd done that. Not single-handedly—the cottage had done its part, the village had done its part. But she'd been the catalyst. She'd had to change before it could bloom.

Lily went and sat among the primroses in the last of the evening light. She thought about

Sophie's words. *You give the love somewhere it belongs.* She thought about Emma holding her close in the bookshop. She thought about Hugh and his love for her sister.

She thought about the month she'd expected to have. And now, the month it had turned into.

'I think I'm staying,' she told the cottage. The primroses. The air smelled of something she was beginning to recognise as home. 'I don't know exactly how, or what it'll look like. But I think this is where I need to be. Near Emma. Near Hugh and Joanna. Near all of this.' She looked at the blooming room. 'Is that all right with you?'

The cottage did not answer. But warmth pressed gently around her, and the primroses nodded in the still air, and Lily Morrison, who had arrived in Lower Thistlewick with a plan, sat among the flowers and understood that she had been quietly and completely rearranged.

Chapter Ten

The following week passed in a blur of wedding preparations and village life, and Lily found herself pulled into the community almost despite herself—or, more accurately, despite the person she'd been when she arrived. That person would have stood at the edge of these preparations, perceiving every happiness as evidence of something wrong. This new version of her—or was it more the old Lily—simply helped.

She assisted Margaret to make more wreaths on Monday. Tuesday, she joined JK to wrap five hundred madeleine favours in small bags tied with white ribbon, a task that JK described as "meditative" and that Lily found was in fact like a meditation, the repetitive folding and tying, the smell of the madeleines, and JK's running commentary on the correct way to tie a bow.

Wednesday morning, Lily helped Vicar Sarah print the wedding programs. The vicar had a printer with a tendency to jam at which meant they spent forty minutes troubleshooting and the rest of the morning talking, easily and honestly, about grief and faith and the ways people found meaning after loss. Vicar Sarah had come to Lower Thistlewick after a difficult period she described without self-pity as "the kind of year that either clarifies everything or destroys you, and the village made sure it was the former." She spoke about the village the way everyone spoke about it—as a place that had chosen them as much as they'd chosen it.

And through all of it, Primrose Cottage bloomed.

Every morning brought new progress in the conservatory. Every plant was now growing.

Primroses in dense clusters, early herbs sending up soft spikes of new growth, the climbing thing at the back wall—whatever it was—putting out tendrils with the purposeful energy of something that had been waiting a long time for permission to get on with it. The garden outside was transforming too, the dormant earth giving way to green in widening patches, the bare borders producing shoots that would be something in a few weeks.

The cottage was warm. The doors opened. The heating worked reliably. The matches caught.

Lily had stopped testing these things. She'd started just living in them.

* * *

On Wednesday afternoon, Mrs Willoughby appeared at the door with her basket and an expression that suggested the visit was not purely social.

'Tea,' she said. 'Mine or yours?'

'Mine.' Lily stepped back. 'I'll make it. The Aga's finally doing what I ask.'

'That's a very good sign.'

They sat in the conservatory, surrounded by the primroses, with cups of tea and a plate of biscuits that Mrs Willoughby had produced from her basket because, as she said, she found it ill-mannered to arrive anywhere without bringing something to eat.

'You've been doing well,' Mrs Willoughby said, looking around at the blooming room. 'The village has noticed. Emma especially.'

'I've been trying. Really trying.'

'I can see that. The cottage can see it.' Mrs Willoughby sipped her tea. 'Which is why I want to talk to you about something, while you're in the right frame of mind to hear it.'

Lily set down her cup. 'All right.'

'You came here with something specific you

were avoiding. You've been doing a great deal of good work—with Hugh, with Emma, with Joanna. You've been honest about your guilt, about the anger, about what you were really here to do. But there's something at the centre of all of it that you haven't fully faced yet.' Mrs Willoughby's gaze was steady and kind. 'Why you weren't there at the end.'

The conservatory was very quiet. Somewhere in the village, someone was hammering something—wedding preparations, probably—and a bird was singing in the garden, and Mrs Willoughby waited.

'I told Hugh,' Lily said carefully. 'That I couldn't face watching her die. That I was frightened. That I was a coward.'

'Yes. You've told that story. But is it the whole story?'

Lily looked at the primroses. She'd been looking at the primroses when she didn't want to look at something, she realised. They'd become a kind of visual refuge in this room.

She made herself stop looking at them and look at Mrs Willoughby instead.

'There was a day,' she said. 'About two months before Sarah died. She'd had a bad week—the treatment was making her very sick, worse than usual, and Hugh had rung me and said I should come, that it wasn't going well. And I came down. I was there for three days.' She stopped.

'Go on.'

'On the third day, Sarah had a good afternoon. She was more herself than she'd been in weeks. We sat in the garden, the three of us—Sarah and Hugh and me—and she was laughing. Making jokes. Giving Hugh terrible advice about the bookshop he was planning. And I thought—' Lily's throat tightened. 'I thought, she's turned a corner. I thought she might actually make it. And I drove home to London feeling hopeful for the first time in months.'

'And?'

'And she deteriorated very quickly after that. The good afternoon was—it was the last real afternoon. The cancer accelerated and within three weeks she could barely speak and within six weeks she was gone.' Lily looked at her hands. 'I was told by the doctors, later, that this can happen. A burst of energy, of apparent wellness, near the end. A last rally. I didn't know that then. I thought she was getting better.'

'And you'd gone home,' Mrs Willoughby said gently.

'I'd gone home. Because I thought she was getting better. And I never came back. Not for that last stretch.' The words were very flat, very still. 'I kept meaning to. I kept saying I'd come the next weekend, or the weekend after. And then Hugh rang me on a Tuesday morning and said it had happened, she was gone, and I'd missed it. Not because I couldn't face being there. Because I'd convinced myself there was more time. Because I'd let hope be a reason to stay away.'

Mrs Willoughby said nothing for a long moment. The bird outside sang on. The hammering continued in the distance.

'And that's what you've never let yourself say out loud,' Mrs Willoughby said at last. 'Not that you were too cowardly to watch her die. But that you were too hopeful. Too human. That you made an ordinary human mistake at the worst possible moment.'

'I left because I thought she was going to be all right.' Lily's voice cracked at the edges. 'I went home happy. I drove away from Sarah's house feeling hopeful and relieved and I never saw her again.'

'Oh, my dear.' Mrs Willoughby's voice was very gentle. 'That's a terrible thing to have been carrying.'

'I told myself I was a coward because that felt like something I deserved. That I stayed away on purpose. That it was a character failing I could be ashamed of. That was easier than the truth.' Lily pressed her hands flat on the table. 'The truth is I just got it wrong. I made a mistake. A normal, human mistake. And she died and I wasn't there and there's nothing to be ashamed of except that I was wrong about something I couldn't have known.'

'Which is worse,' Mrs Willoughby said. 'Because you can't make yourself pay for it. Can't assign blame anywhere. Just live with it.'

'Yes.' Lily's eyes burned. 'If I was a coward, I could hate myself for being a coward. Work on being braver. Earn the forgiveness.

But if I was just—wrong. Just a person who made a normal mistake at an abnormal moment. There's nothing to punish myself for and nothing to improve and nowhere to put the grief except in a box and carry it, and I've never known how to carry it.'

The tears came quietly. Tears that felt more cathartic than sad.

Mrs Willoughby waited.

When Lily was steadier, she said, 'Hugh said Sarah was glad I wasn't there. That she didn't want me to watch her die.'

'That's true. She told me the same thing.'

'Then why does it still feel like failure?'

'Because you loved her.' Mrs Willoughby set down her teacup. 'Because to love someone completely is to want to be there for every part of their life, including the ending. And you weren't there. And that's a real loss—not a moral failure, not a character flaw, but a genuine loss. You lost the chance to say goodbye. To be with her at the end. And that is genuinely, simply sad. And you've never let yourself be sad about it. You've been too busy being angry at yourself.'

Lily looked at the primroses. Deliberately this time, because they were beautiful and because beauty helped.

'What do I do with it?' she asked. Not the question she'd been asking for weeks—the practical question about Hugh and Emma and Joanna. The other question. The older one. 'What do I do with the fact that I wasn't there?'

'You let it be true,' Mrs Willoughby said. 'You let it be something that happened, that you couldn't change, that you didn't choose. You grieve it. And then—you let it go. Not forget it. Not pretend it didn't happen. But stop carrying it as punishment for something you didn't do wrong. Carry it as loss. That's all it ever was.'

That evening, Lily sat at the kitchen table with a sheet of paper and a pen.

She'd been thinking about it since Mrs Willoughby left—about what she hadn't been able to say to Sarah. About the phone calls she'd meant to make. About the goodbye she hadn't had.

She'd been avoiding it for four years. Writing to the dead seemed, in her London life, somewhere between embarrassing and delusional. But she was in a cottage with strong opinions and a conservatory full of primroses, in a village where impossible things happened in the ordinary course of events, and she thought: perhaps this is what the cottage has been waiting for.

She wrote for an hour. She wrote about the last good afternoon in the garden—Sarah laughing, giving Hugh hilarious advice, the hope of it. She wrote about driving home feeling lighter than she had in months, the radio on, the evening sun warm through the car windows, and how she'd thought she was going to be all right. She wrote about Tuesday morning. About what she'd felt when Hugh rang. About the four years since, and how she'd managed her grief by pointing it outward, making it Hugh's fault and Joanna's inconvenience and a moral failing she could prosecute rather than a simple human loss she couldn't fix. The words flowed.

I wasn't there, and I should have been, and I understand now that you'd have said I'm wrong about the 'should have'. But I still wish I'd been there. I still wish I'd held your hand. I still wish the last thing I said to you face-to-face hadn't been goodbye at your garden gate on a Tuesday afternoon when I thought I'd see you again in a fortnight.

I'm going to try to do better with the people who are still here. With Emma and Hugh. With the life you wanted me to have, that I've been refusing to have because having it meant you were really gone.

You were my best friend. You knew me better than anyone. And I think you know that's still true.

She folded the letter, put it in an envelope, and addressed it, simply, to Sarah.

She didn't post it. There was nowhere to post it to. She put it in the box with the baby book and the photograph, and she sat for a long time in the quiet kitchen with the warmth of the Aga at her back, and felt something in her chest that had been clenched for four years very slowly, very carefully, begin to open.

* * *

When Lily went to bed that night, she left the conservatory door open so the smell of the primroses could reach her. She lay in the dark and listened to the village—completely quiet now, no hammering, no voices, just the occasional sound of the millstream carried faintly on the still air.

In the morning, she thought, she'd ring Emma and ask if Saturday's sunrise invitation was still open.

She wanted to watch the day begin.

Chapter Eleven

The realisation that she might want to stay terrified Lily more than anything else that had happened in Lower Thistlewick.

She'd woken on Thursday morning with it sitting clearly at the front of her mind, no longer a vague possibility she considered but an actual intention. She lay in bed for twenty minutes, looking at the ceiling, examining it from various angles.

Staying meant commitment. It would mean dismantling the London life she'd built over fifteen years—the flat, her client list, the version of herself who was good at that kind of work in the city. It meant accepting that Sarah was truly gone and that Lily's future would look nothing like what she'd planned, either the plan she'd made for herself or the one Sarah had made for her. It meant forgiving herself. Actually releasing the burden she'd placed on herself.

That was the terrifying part. She'd been carrying it for so long that she no longer entirely knew who she was without it.

But it also meant this. Being near Emma. Being part of a community that had taken her in despite her worst efforts. Having a cottage that had bloomed around her like a vote of confidence. Having the chance to build something—small, real, made with her hands—that she actually wanted.

The fear and the wanting sat side by side in her chest like two plants growing from the same root. She decided to proceed as if the wanting were going to win, and get up.

* * *

There was one conversation she'd been avoiding.

Not because she didn't know she needed to have it, but because it required the most honesty. With Hugh and Emma, she'd been the one confessing to the wrong she'd done. With Joanna, she'd be confessing to something more complicated: that she'd made her an enemy for no reason except that Joanna was loved.

She walked to Hawthorn Cottage at ten o'clock on Thursday morning. The day was bright and cold, that clear early spring brightness that came before any real warmth, and the village was busy with wedding preparation. Lily walked through it and felt, for the first time a part of it.

Joanna answered the door in jeans and a paint-stained jumper, brushes in hand, looking surprised at first, and then carefully neutral.

' Lily. Is everything all right?'

'Yes. I'm sorry to come without warning. I was hoping we could talk. If you're not in the middle of something.'

'I was in the middle of something, but it can wait.' Joanna glanced at the brushes and then at Lily's expression, and stepped back. 'Come in.'

* * *

Hawthorn Cottage was a comfortable cottage. A large worktable by the window was cluttered with paper, paints and brushes. Emma's books sat on the coffee table, a jumper she'd left behind, draped over a chair.

And on the mantelpiece, where Lily's gaze paused, was a photograph of Sarah.

Not a posed portrait. A candid shot, taken in the garden Lily recognised as Sarah's—the house they'd had before Lower Thistlewick, the one Sarah had planted with such determined optimism for a garden she knew was temporary. Sarah was laughing at something off-camera, head turned, completely unaware of the photograph being taken. She looked well, healthy, full of colour, and totally alive.

Lily stood still.

'Hugh brought that when things became serious between us,' Joanna said, from just behind her. 'He wanted me to know who Sarah was. To understand what Emma had lost and what he'd carried. He said—' she paused. 'He said he didn't want to be with someone who didn't understand the shape of what was missing.'

'That's a very Hugh thing to say.'

'I thought so.' Joanna moved to stand beside her, and they both looked at the photograph. 'She was beautiful.'

'She was. And loud. And absolutely certain she was right about everything, usually correctly. And the best company of anyone I've known in my whole life.' Lily's voice was steady. 'I've spent four years treating her memory as something that needed protecting, and then, from you. And that was wrong. You've been doing the opposite—you've been carrying it with them.'

Joanna was quiet.

'I owe you an apology,' Lily said. 'A specific one.' She turned from the photograph to face Joanna properly. 'I arrived in this village intending to make your life difficult. I'd decided before I met you that you were a threat, an intrusion, someone who was erasing my sister. I ignored your hand at the church. I made things hard for Hugh and Emma by making it clear I disapproved of you. And none of it was about you. You'd done nothing wrong. You were simply present and loved, and I'd decided that was unforgivable.' She took a breath. 'I'm sorry. For how I behaved towards you. It was unkind, and you didn't deserve any of it.'

'You were protecting your sister's memory,' Joanna said quietly. 'In the only way you knew how.'

'That's generous. Too generous, actually.'

'Maybe. But grief makes us—it makes us shape ourselves around the loss in ways that don't always look rational from outside.' Joanna sat on the arm of the sofa. 'I was with someone once who lost a brother. He was never unkind. But he couldn't let anyone be too happy for two years. He'd find a way to dampen it, to bring the mood back to something that matched what he was carrying inside. He didn't know he was doing it. You *knew* you were doing it. That's harder to manage, I think, knowing and still not being able to stop.'

'I'm managing it better now. The cottage has been—instructive.'

Joanna smiled. 'Mrs Willoughby told me about the locked doors. Hawthorn Cottage did something similar with me. I kept finding things I'd put in one place in completely different places. I kept blaming myself for being absent-minded and finally realised that the absent-mindedness was the point—that I wasn't paying attention to my own life, to what I actually wanted, and the cottage was reflecting it back at me in the most literal possible way.'

'What did you want?'

'To stop being careful. I'd been careful for years—careful about everything, careful about getting attached, careful about hoping for anything. And the cottage kept moving things until I stopped being careful about Hugh.' She looked at the photograph on the mantelpiece. 'I was frightened of loving someone who'd lost their wife. Frightened of comparisons, I could never win. Of being always not good enough because the person they'd loved before was someone exceptional.' A pause. 'She was, wasn't she?'

'Completely exceptional,' Lily said. 'Yes.'

'And I'm not trying to be her. I couldn't, and I wouldn't want to. She's Emma's mother and Hugh's wife and the person they both love in a way that is entirely their own and has nothing to do with me.' Joanna looked at Lily directly. 'What I'm doing is different. Loving them in the way I love them, which is my own way, and hoping it's enough.'

'It's enough,' Lily said. 'From the outside—it's genuinely more than enough. Emma is—' She stopped, found the right words. 'Emma is the person she is because of her parents. Both of them. But she's also the person she's becoming because of you. Because you've shown her that love makes room rather than running out. That Sarah's death wasn't the end of all love in her life, just—a terrible loss that made room for something different.' Lily paused. 'I thought loving you was betraying Sarah. But watching Emma, I think not loving

188

you would have been the betrayal. Sarah would have wanted this for her.'

Joanna's eyes were bright. 'That's the kindest thing you could possibly say.'

'I should have said it weeks ago. From the car, probably, before I even got out.' Lily looked at the floor, then back up. 'Can we start again? Properly? I'd like to know you. Not as Hugh's girlfriend or Emma's whatever-you-are. As yourself.'

'I'd like that,' Joanna said. 'Very much. I would like to be your friend.'

* * *

They talked for two hours. Joanna made tea and then coffee and then found biscuits that Emma had hidden in a tin and forgotten about, and they sat in the sitting room and talked in the easy, slightly surprised way of two people discovering they have more in common than they'd expected. Joanna had grown up in the north, moved to London for work, and found London lacking in ways she didn't understand until she left to care for her parents after a divorce.

'How did you end up here?' Lily asked.

'My cousin left me the cottage at a time when I really needed a place to live.

'And then Hugh.'

'Yes, and then Hugh. I stayed in the cottage a long time before I ventured out. He saved me with books and reading.' She missed. 'I had no intention of falling in love.'

They sat quietly for a long moment.

'Will you help me with the wedding?' Lily asked. 'I've been helping Margaret with wreaths, but Emma said there's still work to do on the bridge decoration. I'd like to do it with you, if that's all right.'

Joanna looked surprised, then pleased. 'I'd like that.'

'Tomorrow morning? The arch needs more greenery, and I've been putting it off because doing it alone seemed like hard work.'

'I'll be there.'

* * *

Friday brought Sophie and Daniel back to the village.

They arrived mid-morning, and by the time Lily and Joanna had finished at the bridge later that afternoon, Mrs Willoughby had organised dinner at Rose Cottage—'casual, just come'—and so they came. All of them. Sophie and Daniel, Dimity and Vivian, Hugh and Joanna, Emma, Margaret, JK, Alf, Vicar Sarah, and Lily.

Sophie greeted Lily warmly. 'We were rooting for you,' she said, holding Lily's hands briefly. 'Mrs Willoughby gave us updates. Very proper updates—just "progress is being made"—but in a very encouraging tone.'

'She's been—wonderful,' Lily said. 'The cottage too. And Emma.'

'Emma's extraordinary,' Sophie agreed. 'She taught me about the flower language that your sister had taught her.'

They swapped cottage stories; Sophie told the story of the amaryllis Daniel had found the morning after their worst night: it bloomed overnight, in February, in a cold conservatory. Daniel described the locked bathroom door on the morning he'd been about to leave, which had simply refused to open until he knocked, and Sophie answered from the other side.

'It kept putting us in the same place,' Sophie said. 'We kept trying to be separate—sleeping in separate rooms, avoiding mealtimes—and the cottage kept arranging things so we had to actually face each other. It was very undignified.'

'Primrose Cottage locked me in the

hallway,' Lily said. 'For the better part of a whole afternoon. I sat on the floor and cried.'

'That's cottage therapy,' Daniel said. 'Uncomfortable, but effective.'

'Mrs Willoughby hinted you were thinking about staying in the village.'

'I've decided. I just haven't said it out loud yet to anyone who matters.' Lily looked around the room—at Emma, who was demonstrating her wedding walk yet again, at Hugh watching Joanna laugh at something Dimity had said, at the whole warm gathering in the sitting room. 'I'm staying. Long-term rental of Primrose Cottage. And I'm thinking about a shop—small, plants and handmade things, locally sourced. The space next to Chapter & Verse is empty.'

'Oh, Emma will be absolutely delighted,' Sophie said immediately.

She was. When Hugh mentioned it, Emma put down her glass and went completely still for one moment, absorbing it, and then said: 'You're staying? Actually staying? Not just—'

'Actually staying,' Lily confirmed.

Emma's face broke into an enormous smile. 'Mum said you'd find your way here.'

'She was usually right.'

'Always,' Emma said. 'Infuriatingly so.' Lily closed her eyes as her niece's arms went around her. 'I'm so pleased, Aunty Lily.'

Later, after dinner, Hugh pulled Lily aside into Mrs Willoughby's kitchen while the others continued around the sitting room fire.

'Joanna told me you had a good chat,' he said.

'I hope that was all right.'

'More than all right.' He leaned against the counter. 'She said you told her Sarah would have liked her.'

'She would have.'

'That means everything to Joanna. And to

me.' He was quiet for a moment. 'I want to tell you something. About the end. About what Sarah said.'

'Hugh—'

'Let me.' He looked at his hands. 'In the last week, when she could still talk, she said to me, "When Lily comes, and she will come eventually, make sure she knows I was glad she didn't watch me die. Make sure she knows I wanted her to remember me as I was. And make sure she knows I forgave her before there was anything to forgive".' He looked up. 'I should have told you that four years ago. I was too angry and too raw. But it's what she said. Word for word. I've been carrying it since.'

Lily stood very still. 'She wanted me to remember her as she was,' she said quietly. 'I understand that now.'

'That afternoon in the garden. When you thought she was getting better.' Hugh's voice was gentle. 'She knew. She could feel herself rallying. She told me that afternoon that she was glad you'd seen her like that—laughing, like herself. She said, "That's the version Lily needs to hold onto. Not the rest of it." She sent you home on purpose, Lily. So you'd have that.'

The kitchen was very quiet. Somewhere in the wall, the cottage's pipes made a small, contented sound.

'She sent me home on purpose,' Lily said.

'She always knew exactly what she was doing.'

'Infuriatingly so,' Lily repeated Emma's words.

Hugh smiled.

'Stay,' he said. 'Build your shop. Be part of Emma's life. Be part of all of this. Sarah wanted that for you. I want it for you. And this village is very good at making things happen that need to happen.'

'I know,' Lily said. 'I've been noticing that.'

She walked home through the dark village under a sky that had cleared to brilliant stars. She stopped on the bridge and looked into the millstream below, the water catching the moonlight in moving pieces. Eight hundred years of water running past the same stone, and still going.

She thought about what Hugh had said. About Sarah sending her home on purpose, giving her the memory she needed to carry rather than the ending she couldn't have survived. About love as a decision made even in those last difficult weeks—the decision to protect Lily from something Sarah could protect her from, at the cost of the goodbye they should have had.

It made her cry, standing on the bridge. This

felt like the last of something—the last of the burden she had created. Not the end of the grief. But the end of her guilt.

She wiped her face and walked on.

Primrose Cottage was warm when she got home. The conservatory was glowing faintly with the phosphorescent quality that pale flowers had in moonlight, and she stood in the doorway and looked at it for a long time.

'She sent me home on purpose,' she told the cottage. The flowers. The room that had fought her and then, slowly, accepted her and then, slowly, bloomed around her. 'Did you know that?'

The primroses nodded in the still air.

Lily decided to take that as a yes.

Chapter Twelve

The final days before the wedding were filled with a burst of unseasonably warm weather and an explosion of spring flowers. The village transformed—the green became a carpet of daffodils and primroses, cherry trees bloomed along the lanes, and everywhere Lily looked, colour and life.

Primrose Cottage had become a riot of blooms. The conservatory was so full of primroses that Lily could barely walk through it. The garden outside was equally spectacular—thousands of pale yellow flowers creating drifts of colour against the stone walls, wisteria trailing down the walls and from empty Lavender Cottage two doors up, the overpowering fragrance of lavender in bloom.

'The cottage approves,' Mrs Willoughby

said when she visited on Monday. 'Look at this! I've never seen Primrose Cottage bloom like this. Not ever!'

'I'm trying to heal. Properly heal, not just pretend.'

'It shows.' Mrs Willoughby touched a primrose gently. 'You're staying?'

'Yes. If the offer's still open, I'd like to take Primrose Cottage long-term. Maybe Lower Thistlewick needs a gift shop.'

'The village would love that. And the empty shop next to Chapter & Verse has been vacant for months. Hugh's landlord would probably give you a good deal.'

They spent the morning discussing what was needed. By lunchtime, Lily's head was spinning, but her heart felt light.

* * *

On Wednesday, Fern and Callum arrived in the village for final preparations. They arrived mid-morning, Fern's car packed with wedding things and Callum carrying what looked like an alarming amount of ribbon.

'We're here!' Fern announced on the village green, where people had gathered to help with setup. 'Who needs a job? We have a million things to do and two days to do them!'

The village responded with the efficiency of a well-rehearsed production. Alf and Hugh erected the arch on the bridge where the ceremony would take place. Dimity and Vivian strung garlands between lampposts. Margaret and Lily distributed wreaths to all the cottages. Emma and several other village children scattered around placing lanterns along the paths.

JK appeared with a trolley full of madeleines in their little bags. 'Five hundred! I may never make another madeleine as long as I live. But they are beautiful, no?'

'They're perfect,' Fern assured her. 'Everything's perfect. I can't believe you've all done this for us.'

'The village takes care of its own,' Mrs Willoughby said. 'And you're one of ours now. You and Callum both.'

By evening, the village looked like something from a fairy tale. Flowers everywhere, lanterns ready to be lit, the bridge decorated with ivy and primroses and early roses. The green was set up with chairs and tables for the reception, fairy lights strung overhead, a space cleared for dancing later.

'It's magical,' Sophie said, standing with Daniel and surveying the scene. 'Properly magical.'

'That's Lower Thistlewick for you,' Joanna said. She stood with Hugh, his arm around her waist, both of them watching Emma run about with the other children. 'The village believes in magic. So magic happens.'

That evening, the whole village gathered at The Old Swan for an impromptu celebration dinner. Alf outdid himself with food—proper pub fare in massive servings. Fern and Callum sat at the centre table, radiating happiness, surrounded by the community that had adopted them in February.

Lily sat at a table with Emma, Joanna, Hugh, Dimity, and Vivian.

At one point, Emma whispered to Lily: 'I'm glad you're staying. I do like having you here.'

'I'm glad too.'

'Mum told me you would need looking after.' Emma smiled. 'I was eight. I didn't really understand. But now I do. And I'm glad you're here so I can look after you properly.'

Lily's eyes filled with tears. 'You're very wise for twelve.'

'I've had a lot of practice.' Emma's tone

was matter-of-fact. 'But we're both doing better now, aren't we? You and me.'

'Yes, sweetheart. We truly are.'

Chapter Thirteen

May Day dawned clear and bright—perfect wedding weather.

Lily woke early in Primrose Cottage, surrounded by blooming primroses, and took a moment to appreciate the cottage. She dressed carefully in the outfit she'd bought specially for the occasion—a spring dress in lavender, comfortable shoes for standing, a light jacket in case the weather turned. Then she walked to Hawthorn Cottage, where she'd promised to help Emma get ready.

Emma answered the door in her dressing gown, hair still damp from the shower, eyes sparkling with excitement. 'Aunt Lily! Come in, come in! Joanna's doing my hair and I need you to tell me if the dress looks right!'

The next hour was a chaos of hair styling and dress adjustments and Emma's non-stop questions about what would happen at the ceremony. Joanna moved through it all, braiding Emma's dark hair with ribbon and fresh forget-me-nots, helping her into the bridesmaid dress that Fern had chosen—simple and beautiful, covered in embroidered flowers.

'You look perfect,' Lily said honestly.

'Mum would love this dress,' Emma said, examining herself in the mirror. 'She always said forget-me-nots were the best flowers because they mean true love and remembering people. That's why we chose them. So Mum could be part of the day too, even though she's not here.'

'Your mum is here,' Joanna said softly. 'In you. In how kind you are, how thoughtful. You're so much like her, Emma.'

'Really?'

'Really. Hugh's told me so many stories. And I can see Sarah in you—the way you care about people, the way you notice when someone's sad, the way you always try to help.' Joanna tied the last ribbon. 'Your mum would be incredibly proud of you.'

'She'd be proud of you too,' Emma said to Lily. 'For coming here. For staying.'

'When did you get so wise?'

'I've always been wise. You just weren't listening before.' But Emma grinned. 'Come on. We're going to be late.'

They walked to the village green together—Emma between them, holding both their hands, flower crown perfect in her braided hair. Hugh was waiting by the bridge, looking smart in his suit, and his expression when he saw Emma brought happy tears to Lily's eyes.

'My beautiful girl,' he said, voice thick. 'Your mum would be so proud. I'm proud of you, sweetheart.'

'I know, Dad. I can feel her.'

The village began gathering. Chairs filled with people—villagers, Fern and Callum's family and friends who'd travelled from elsewhere. Mrs Willoughby marshalled everyone. Margaret made final adjustments to flowers. JK fretted over the madeleines displayed on the gift table.

At a quarter to noon, Vicar Sarah took her place on the bridge. The village quietened. Emma took her position at the start of the procession route, clutching a basket of primrose petals to scatter.

And then, Fern emerged from Rose Cottage.

She looked radiant. A simple white dress covered in embroidered flowers, hair loose with blooms woven through it, barefoot on the grass. She walked slowly across the green, her feet bare, and everywhere she stepped, flowers bloomed—violets and primroses and tiny white blossoms that hadn't been there a moment before.

'Is that real?' someone from away whispered.

'This is Lower Thistlewick,' someone else responded. 'Everything's real here.'

Emma walked ahead of Fern, scattering primrose petals with solemn concentration. Behind Fern came Mrs Willoughby, beaming with pride, and Fern's parents looking slightly overwhelmed by the magic of it all.

Callum waited on the bridge, grinning.

The ceremony was perfect. Vicar Sarah spoke about love and choice and the daily magic of loving someone. Fern and Callum exchanged vows they'd written themselves—promises to choose each other daily, to weather storms together, to build a life of ordinary and extraordinary moments.

When Vicar Sarah pronounced them married and they kissed, the village and guests erupted in cheers. Church bells rang. And the flowers around the bridge—which had been plentiful before—suddenly multiplied, creating drifts of colour and scent that defied every natural law.

'Magic,' Lily whispered to Joanna.

'Always,' Joanna whispered back.

Chapter Fourteen

The reception on the village green was everything a wedding celebration should be—food and wine and dancing and joy. Alf had outdone himself with the catering. Margaret's cake was a masterpiece. JK's madeleines were the perfect sweet touch and appreciated by all who sampled them.

Lily was pulled into dance after dance. With Emma, giggling and spinning. With Hugh, who thanked her quietly for being there with them. With Alf, who subjected her to more terrible jokes. With Callum, who told her earnestly that the village had the best people in the world, and he was grateful to be part of it.

She was catching her breath at a table near the millstream when she became aware of someone sitting down uninvited in the chair beside her.

'You're Lily.' Not a question. He had a glass of wine and the look of a man who was quietly relieved to have found somewhere to sit. Dark hair, a few threads of grey at the temples. 'Callum's been talking about you. The aunt who came to sort things out and stayed instead.'

'That's a generous version,' Lily said.

'I'm Patrick. Callum's cousin.' He held out a hand, and she shook it. His grip was brief, but firm. 'I've moved from Bristol. He's been suggesting I move here since Fern discovered the village.'

'You're going to stay in the village?' Lily narrowed her eyes. 'In a cottage?'

He looked at the village—the green, the bridge still hung with flowers, the light going golden over the honey-stone cottages. Something in his expression was difficult to read. Not unhappiness, exactly. Something deeper than that.

'I'm starting at Ringwood Secondary in September,' he said. 'Head of English. Callum mentioned a cottage. Lavender something.'

'Lavender Cottage.' Lily glanced towards the far end of the lane, two doors from Primrose Cottage, where the cottage sat quiet behind its gate. 'Another of Mrs Willoughby's. It's been waiting a while, I think.'

Something in her tone made him look at her properly for the first time. She looked back and found his eyes were very direct, the eyes of someone who paid close attention to things and was possibly regretting sitting here now.

'Waiting?' he repeated.

'The cottages here tend to find the people they need,' Lily said. 'And vice versa.'

He looked at her as if he wasn't sure whether she was serious. Then he looked at the bridge, where Fern and Callum were dancing, where the flowers hadn't faded in four hours of warmth and music, where the village was gathered in celebration, and the magic of the place was simply sitting openly in the late afternoon light, not bothering to explain itself.

'Right,' he said quietly with a nod, as if adding something to an internal list.

They sat for a while in silence. Below them, the millstream ran on, unhurried and constant.

'Ringwood Secondary,' Lily said. 'That's where Emma goes.'

'Hugh's daughter? Callum mentioned her.' Something shifted in his expression—the complicated thing resolving briefly into something clearer. 'He said she was remarkable.'

'She is.' Lily looked towards the dance floor, where Emma was currently attempting to teach JK a reel with mixed results. 'She'll probably review your first lesson for the school newsletter.'

Patrick almost smiled. It looked like a thing he'd been out of practice with. 'That's terrifying.'

'It should be. She has very high standards.'

Fern appeared then, flushed and laughing, pulling Callum behind her, and the moment dissolved into introductions and wedding energy, and Patrick was absorbed back into the celebration. But once, across the green, he caught Lily's eye, and she looked away first.

She wasn't entirely sure why.

* * *

As sunset approached, Fern found Lily sitting at one of the tables, catching her breath.

'Tired?' Fern asked, settling beside her.

'Happily so. It's been a perfect day.'

'It has. Thank you for helping with decorations. And for being here. Emma's talked about you non-stop this week—how glad she is you're staying.'

'I'm glad too. I came here angry and lost. The village gave me back myself.'

'That's what it does.' Fern looked around at the celebration—people dancing, children running about, the community in full celebration mode. 'When I first arrived in February, I was running away. Terrified of commitment, convinced I was too strange to deserve love. And the village just held me. Let me figure it out. Gave me space to become brave.'

'One of the cottages helped you?'

Fern shook her head. 'I camped in a tent in the field over there. Every morning, I'd wake to new flowers, as if the village was saying we see you, we accept you, you belong here. It took me three weeks to believe it. To stop running and choose to stay.' Fern smiled. 'I think that's the village's real magic. It shows you that belonging is possible. That community is real.

That you don't have to face everything alone.'

'I'm beginning to understand that.'

They sat together watching the sunset paint the sky pink and gold. Around them, Lower Thistlewick celebrated—dancing and laughing and living together, embracing joy without forgetting sorrow, honouring the past whilst building the future.

And Lily, for the first time in four years, felt at home.

Epilogue

Two weeks after the wedding, Lily signed the lease on the empty shop next to Chapter & Verse.

She did it on a Tuesday morning with a pen borrowed from Hugh, and Mrs Willoughby as a witness, and when she put the pen down, she sat for a moment in the bare space that would be Primrose & Thyme and felt certain that this was the right thing to do. Her colleagues in London thought she was crazy. She smiled.

It had all moved quickly, in the way things moved in Lower Thistlewick when the village had made up its mind. The landlord had been surprisingly amenable. Hugh had appeared with a measuring tape the same afternoon. Joanna had helpful opinions about the colour of the shelving. Emma had drawn up a list of what the window display should contain. Lily was beginning to see more of Sarah in Emma every day.

By the end of the first week, the walls were painted. By the end of the second, the shelves were up.

Lily spent her mornings painting and her afternoons sourcing stock—local potters, the lavender farm, a woman in Upper Thistlewick who made extraordinary pressed-flower cards, Joanna's paintings at the back wall where the light fell perfectly. She went to bed tired each night with paint in her hair and the satisfaction of someone building a new life. A life she already loved.

And with her family close by.

On Thursday afternoon in the second week, Lily saw the car.

She was standing on a stepladder hanging a shelf bracket when an unfamiliar car came slowly down the lane and stopped outside

Lavender Cottage. She watched from the window; the car was loaded—boxes on the back seat, a bag on the passenger side, with the look of someone moving rather than visiting. Her breath caught when the driver's door opened, and Patrick got out.

It was a clear May afternoon, wisteria was in full bloom over the gate, the lavender border already showing purple, everything looking beautiful in the way the village always welcomed someone. He stared at the cottage for quite a while.

Lily came down from the stepladder; the shelf bracket could wait, and she was going to be his neighbour-ish. The memory of the wedding—their easy rapport by the millstream, the almost smile—and she picked up her jacket.

Patrick was lifting a box from the back seat when Lily crossed the lane.

'You made it,' she said.

He looked up. His smile was immediate, and the expression in his eyes held something that warmed her. 'Lily. Hello.' He set the box down on the low wall. 'You're—' He looked at the shop behind her, the freshly painted sign in the window. 'Is that yours?'

'It is. I signed the lease two weeks ago.' She nodded at the cottage. 'Callum said you'd be coming this week.'

'He wasn't wrong.' Patrick looked at Lavender Cottage, then back at her. He looked tired. 'Small village,' he said.

'Very.' She looked at the boxes in the car. 'Do you need a hand?'

He started to say no—she could see it forming—and then he looked at the number of boxes. 'That would be a fabulous help.'

The cottage smelled of lavender and old stone and the sunshine of a south-facing room in May. Patrick set things down without unpacking, finding places for boxes on various surfaces, and Lily left him to it.

When the car was empty, they stood in the small hallway, and he said, 'Thank you. I'd have managed, but it would have taken considerably longer.'

'The village feeds you when you arrive,' Lily said. 'JK will appear tomorrow with madeleines. Mrs Willoughby will come this afternoon with something sustaining, like a casserole. Alf from the pub will tell you a terrible joke by Friday at the latest.'

His face lightened; not quite a smile, but in the same direction. 'Forewarned,' he said. 'Thank you.'

Lily nodded. 'I know the routine. Also, the pub does a good pie, if you don't feel like cooking tonight.'

'That sounds like a good idea.'

'Well, I'd better get back to work,' she said,

strangely not wanting to leave.'

'Thanks again for your help, ' Patrick said. 'I owe you.'

Lily left him to his unpacking and crossed back to the shop. She stood at the window for a moment, thinking, wondering. Then she looked at the shelf brackets she still needed to hang, the arrangement she'd been planning for the front display, the business she was building from the ground up in the village she now called home.

She was *not* thinking about Patrick Doyle.

The bunch of lavender she'd put in a jar on the windowsill that morning had acquired three more stems, and the smell of it was warm and sweet.

Lily looked at it for a long moment.

She was pleased to see Patrick had moved to the village and wondered if he, too, was here to heal. She picked up her drill and went back to the shelf brackets.

Mayday Magic… coming in May is the sixth book in the beloved Enchanted Village series—a story about the courage it takes to choose your own life, and the person who helps you realise you already have.

Patrick Doyle was supposed to be something brilliant. His family had chosen his profession before he'd even finished school—medicine, law, anything worthy of their cleverest son. Instead, he followed his heart and became an English teacher. And for a long time, that was enough.

Then came the year that broke him.

Now Patrick has moved to the Cotswolds, his books packed in boxes and his faith in himself left behind, to take up a teaching post in a quiet market town and a cottage in a village. But Lavender Cottage has been waiting for him.

As May unfolds across the village, Lily

Morrison starts her new shop and watches Patrick Doyle move quietly through it, slowly coming to understand himself. Can she help him see that maybe he made the right choice?

The village does its work. It always does.

Print: https://annieseatonstore.ecwid.com/MayDay-Magic-p826785524

eBook: https://books2read.com/u/m29ZkR

Direct eBook: https://payhip.com/b/7JBAP

Annie Seaton

Scan to subscribe to Annie's newsletter for sneak previews, weekly deals and early information about her upcoming books

SCAN ME

www.annieseaton.net

Annie's Print Store

Awards

2024: Finalist – Romantic suspense category, RUBY award for *From Across the Sea.*

2023: Winner - Long contemporary novel category, RUBY award for *Larapinta.*

2023: Finalist - Australian Romance Readers Awards for *Kakadu Dawn,* the sixth and final book in the Porter Sisters series.

2018 and 2020: Finalist - for the NZ KORU Award.

2017: Winner - Best Established Author of the Year AUSROM

2017: Winner - Author of the Year 2016, 2017, 2018, 2019: Longlisted - Sisters in Crime Davitt Awards

2016: Finalist - Book of the Year, Long Romance, RWA Ruby Awards for *Kakadu Sunset*

2015: Winner - Best Established Author of the Year AUSROM

2014 AUSROM - Best Established Author, Ausrom Readers' Choice.

www.ingramcontent.com/pod-product-compliance
Lightning Source LLC
Chambersburg PA
CBHW032011050726
47590CB00006B/2128